The Bishop's Legacy

Book III, World of Shadows

By Lincoln Cole

This is a work of fiction. Names, characters, organizations, places, events, and incidents are either products of the author's imagination or used fictitiously. Any resemblance to actual persons, living or dead, or actual events is purely coincidental.

No part of this work may be reproduced, or stored in a retrieval system, or transmitted in any form or by any means, electronic, mechanical, photocopying, recording, or otherwise, without written permission of the publisher.

Published by Lincoln Cole, Columbus, 2017
Lincoln@LincolnCole.net
www.LincolnCole.net

Cover Design by M.N. Arzu
www.mnarzuauthor.com

"Then shall he say also unto them on the left hand, Depart from me, ye cursed, into everlasting fire, prepared for the devil and his angels:"

Matthew 25:41

Prologue

The dying man's eyes slipped closed and he took another rasping breath. Debra couldn't believe that this was happening and knew she wasn't going to be able to save him. The hospital lights flickered around her and she let out a sob.

"Please. Please, stay with me."

The grip on her hand loosened as his life ebbed away. He was about to die, she realized, and more tears streamed down her cheeks.

"Someone please!" she screamed at the empty emergency room around her. "This man needs help! Please! I don't know what to do!"

His eyes suddenly shot open, and his grip on her hand tightened almost enough to hurt. She jerked back, but he didn't let go.

He leaned his head up the tiniest bit from the floor, looked her squarely in the eyes, and mumbled something to her.

Then, his eyes slipped closed and his head fell back to the floor. The blood stopped pumping out of his neck.

She knelt there for what felt like forever in shock and confusion. He was no longer dying, she knew: he was dead.

That wasn't all, though. He had spoken to her, and the word floated in her thoughts just out of reach, difficult to focus on. It took her a second to realize what it was the man had whispered to her with his final breath.

Run.

She never got the chance.

Chapter 1

"Two more incidents this morning," Frieda said. Even over the phone Arthur could hear the exhaustion in her voice. He doubted she had slept much in the last couple of days. "My phone has been buzzing constantly and I feel like for each fire we put out two more pop up."

"You're kidding," Arthur replied. "How much damage can these kids do?"

He had his phone on speaker and resting on his lap. He had tried putting it up on the dash but it slid around too much and he had to scramble to catch it. The car jostled and bounced on the dirt road, and he continually had to adjust it to keep it in position.

He would have asked Niccolo to hold it for him, but that would have been a complete waste of his breath. At this point he wasn't willing to ask the priest to help with much of anything.

Father Niccolo Paladina sat in the passenger seat of his rental car, quiet and lethargic as he stared out the window at nothing. There were only trees and foliage around them as distraction, Arthur knew that his thoughts were internal anyway.

He was withdrawn and somber, much more diminutive than he had when they first began this mission. Only a few weeks since the events in Everett, Washington had wrecked him spiritually and emotionally.

Staring out that car window had been the only thing he had done for the last several hours of driving. He hadn't spoken since they fled their hotel room in California after the events in the shipyard.

Arthur was driving them through the forest outside his hidden cabin in Colorado. It was an uneven road and difficult to navigate, but he had driven down this way a thousand times before.

His biggest problem right now was that a storm had passed through sometime in the preceding days while they were hunting down the Bishop, so he had to drive around some fallen debris, including a huge tree that blocked one section of the road. This rental wasn't made for off-road driving, and he was worried that they would get stuck.

"I wish I was kidding, Arthur," Frieda continued. "One twelve-year-old boy attacked a supermarket with some sort of windstorm and injured over a dozen people. Another little girl set a building on fire."

"Are you sure they were Leopold's children? Starting fires doesn't really seem to fit his MO."

"Positive they were. She started the fire with her fingers. Both of the kids were in his notes we recovered from the shipyard."

"No major psychic abilities?"

"Not these ones. At least not that we saw. Charles Greathouse rounded up the little girl without much trouble. The building was unoccupied and the injuries in the market are being blamed on freak coincidence. Neither even was difficult to tidy up," Frieda replied. "Nobody saw anything out of the ordinary and the events were unrelated."

"Looks like you're getting lucky."

"How long until that luck runs out? I think this is only the tip of the iceberg. Things are about to get a lot crazier."

"How so?"

"We found thirty other names on the list."

"Thirty?" he asked. "That's insane."

"Tell me about it."

"How did so many kids go missing without anyone noticing?"

"I wish I knew, Arthur. That's not all. There were mentions of other kids that aren't included in the Bishop's plans or listed in the notes with names. We don't know where they are or what they are planning, but it looks like there could be as many as seven more kids unaccounted for."

"Any leads you can give me? Where should I check first?"

"I'll tell you as soon as the Church tells me," she said. "They are reading through the Bishop's notes and trying to make sense of it all. Right now, they are keeping their cards close to the chest. If I had anything to offer you, I would."

"Alright. I guess I'll just play it by ear, then."

"Don't feel too bad. That's what I'm going to be doing, too. How long will it take you to get there?"

"A day and a half to two, give or take. I'm hoping to drive straight through."

"Let me know as soon as you cross the state line into Ohio."

"I will. And you let me know if you hear anything else from the Church. I want to get out ahead of this if we can."

"Will do. Take care, Arthur."

"You too."

He hung up the phone and dropped it into the cup holder between the seats. The interior of the car fell silent, the only sound the tires grinding rocked the narrow and winding dirt road. A gust of wind pushed the car a little bit off the road, forcing Arthur to correct and keep them on the path. A little stronger of a gust and they would have been split into a tree.

Maybe the storm hadn't completely passed after all.

"We're almost there," he said. "Couple more minutes and we'll be at the cabin to check on Desiree."

He wasn't really expecting a reply from the priest, and Niccolo didn't offer one. Instead, he kept staring out the window with the same moody expression on his face. Arthur was wondering, and not for the first time, if the priest might be more of a liability on this mission than a help.

It was late in the afternoon and would be dark by the time they reached his cabin. When they first left California he had considered skipping this trip entirely and driving straight through to Ohio, but he needed to collect some supplies and check in on Desiree before they went to deal with Jeremy.

He also wanted to make sure that Desiree hadn't burned his cabin to the ground. He was pretty sure she wouldn't, but it was still a chance. Honestly, if she had, he wouldn't have blamed her.

He played back his conversation with Frieda in his mind. She was scrambling to do damage control around the country from all of the attacks. He could hardly believe things were happening so quickly. Already four incidents in only a day.

Either the Bishop had triggered his soldiers around the country before he died or, more likely, Jeremy had seized control in the power vacuum and was starting the plan on his own. If Frieda was right, then there could be dozens more children out there planning horrific acts of violence all around the country.

The Bishop might be dead, but his legacy was alive and well.

✳✳✳

Arthur was relieved when they finally pulled up to his cabin and it was still standing. It still hadn't begun storming, but he could feel the heavy rain coming just from the taste of the air. They needed to be on their way out of here before the storm caught them and trapped them.

Luckily, they were a little bit ahead of schedule and there was still some light left in the day. It was a relief to get out of the cramped and uncomfortable rental car and stretch his legs. With Niccolo's incessant silence it was beginning to feel more like a funeral hearse than a Chevrolet.

He had known this was going to be a long and cumbersome drive with the distracted priest, he just hadn't known how withdrawn and quiet the man would become. He had hoped that by now the priest would have gotten over the horrible events at the shipyard, but if anything he was only getting worse.

Not that he blamed Niccolo for the somber attitude. The priest was still dealing with the turmoil of the last several days and everything that came with it. It would be difficult to come to terms with what he had done: he had killed someone, and even though the shooting was justified and unavoidable, it was still a lot to deal with.

To be honest, Arthur could hardly believe that Niccolo had pulled the trigger to end the Bishop's life. He could only imagine what the priest must be feeling right about now. Niccolo had shot someone, a Bishop no less. It was something Arthur wouldn't have expected from the mild-mannered priest in a thousand years.

Even with the death being self-defense, it was weighing on the Priest's soul.

What made it worse, however, was that they had just left. Arthur was used to leaving the scene of a crime with dead bodies, but for Niccolo it meant they were avoiding the responsibility. The guilt, shame, and fear of getting caught were no doubt weighing him down.

Still, he didn't have time to worry about Niccolo right now. The priest would have to deal with it on his own, because they were in a hurry.

He turned the car off and then peered up at the front of his cabin. The curtains were pulled closed, but he could still see some light spilling out of the front room. Arthur sighed in relief, because part of him had been afraid that when they made it back here Desiree would already be gone. He'd left her a car and keys as well as a map to make it back to the main road.

They had only been gone a few days, but he had no idea what she had gotten up to while they were out hunting down the Bishop. He wanted to make sure that she knew the Bishop was dead, though, and that she could go home.

"I'll go check up on Desiree and then we can get back on the road. Do you want to stay here or come inside with me?"

Niccolo didn't respond, just continued staring out that window with that same vacant expression on his face. If he even heard Arthur he gave no sign. Arthur waited a moment, seeing if he would respond, and then shrugged.

"Suit yourself. Guess you'll be waiting. Don't go anywhere, I'll be right back."

Niccolo gave him the faintest nod without looking for him. He closed the car door and strode up to the front entrance of the cabin. He considered just heading inside – after all, it was his cabin – and then changed his mind. He wasn't sure whether Desiree knew they were here, and he didn't want to startle her.

He knocked on the door.

He heard scrambling from inside and what sounded like glass breaking. He winced, even though there wasn't anything of actual value in the entire place. A second later and the door of the cabin cracked open a couple of inches.

The barrel of a shotgun greeted him.

Not the tranquilizer dart gun he'd left her with, he noted, but a full-on twelve-gauge shotgun. He had left her the keys to his cabin, but he hadn't really thought she would go poking around, much less find his armory.

He kept quite a few guns locked away in his room, and they were hidden behind a secret door that he realized wasn't as secret as he'd originally thought. That, or maybe she was a better sleuth than he'd given her credit for.

"Um…hey?" he said.

Her expression softened when she saw it was him and she lowered the gun.

"You scared the hell out of me," she admonished him, opening the door wider. She put a hand on her heart. "Thing's beating a mile a minute. Do you know what time it is?"

"No clue. Why, what time is it?"

"I have no idea," she admitted. "Late. I know that much."

She was still blocking the doorway, shaking her

head in annoyance. Arthur waited for a second for her to move out of his way, but she didn't.

"Can I come in?" he asked, only the barest hint of sarcasm in his voice. "It is my cabin, after all."

"Oh yeah, sure. Sorry."

She stepped out of the way to let him through. Arthur walked in past her and nearly gasped in surprise. He saw that the interior of his cabin was impeccably clean and organized. In fact, everything was in perfect order except for what looked like a tea cup that had smashed on the floor in front of his couch.

A fire burned pleasantly in the fireplace and it looked...

Cozy.

He hated it.

Desiree, apparently, could tell. She fidgeted and cleared her throat.

"I had to do something while I was here alone," she said. "And I clean when I'm worrying or nervous about something. This place gets creepy at night when I'm here alone and I needed some way to occupy myself."

"I can see that."

"Any news? You guys were gone for several days."

He hesitated; how much, he wondered, should he tell her? Arthur honestly didn't know how much the Church would want her to know, but after a moment he decided that honesty was the best option.

After all, if the Church hadn't let her down with its secrecy and lies, then none of them would be in this situation.

"Bishop Glasser won't be a problem for you any longer."

"What do you mean? Did you catch him?"

"He's dead."

"Dead?"

A mixed expression of relief, trepidation, and shock flashed across her face. It was replaced with something that seemed a little bit like regret. He could understand and sympathize: she'd been building herself up for the last several days to the realization that she might actually have to meet the Bishop face-to-face again.

She wouldn't have to now, but his being dead also meant she wouldn't be able to. The thought of meeting him probably terrified her, to be sure, but it also excited her. It would be her chance to face her abuser head on and move past it.

Now, though, she would never get that chance.

"I thought the plan was to turn him over to the Church for justice?"

"It was the plan," Arthur agreed. "That was why we went there to begin with, but things took a turn. Shooting him was self-defense."

"So, you had no choice but to kill him?"

"Not me. I didn't do it."

"Then who did?"

"Niccolo."

"Woah, wait, what? Niccolo, the priest, killed Leopold?"

"It wasn't intentional and Leopold gave him no other choice. He refused to give up until Niccolo panicked and pulled the trigger."

She blew out a breath. "How's he taking it?"

"About as well as we might expect."

"That's too bad."

"I know."

"Do you want some tea?" she asked. "I can make some more. Where is Niccolo?"

"In the car. No thanks, for the tea."

"Ah. He needs alone time."

"Yeah."

Arthur found it somewhat strange that he was having this conversation with Desiree at all. After all, only a few days ago she had been his prisoner and locked in the basement until Niccolo forced him to free her. Trusting her hadn't been easy, but that wasn't her fault nor her problem.

It was his.

It didn't feel like a few days, though: it felt like months had passed since he'd first kidnapped Desiree at her home to protect her from the Bishop. So much had happened since he left here with Niccolo that it felt like an entirely different world.

It had been the right choice to free Desiree and he was glad Niccolo had demanded it of him. He wasn't one for trusting people, certainly not someone who had no reason to trust him back, but Desiree was an incredibly friendly and forgiving person.

It made her all the more special since she had every reason not to be. Without Niccolo's influence she would probably still be locked down in the basement waiting for him to let her go.

"He hasn't been willing to talk to me – or anyone – since it happened."

"I guess I get it," she said. "That's a lot to deal with, especially for someone like him. I doubt he could handle something like that even if he wasn't a priest, but in this case it goes against everything he stands for."

"I know. I just wish there was something to say to make him feel better."

"There isn't. I doubt he would want to feel better

even if he could. Time is what he needs."

"That's something we don't have."

"Then keep him busy. If he doesn't have time to think, he won't have time worry about it."

"Maybe. In either case, his problem is because your problems are dealt with. Leopold can't do anything else to you anymore. You're free."

"So, it's over? It's really over?"

"Yes. Well, mostly. The children that he was gathering are still out there somewhere. We're working to find them, but the Bishop didn't exactly leave a guide about where we would find them. They are scattered all across the country and the best we can do is chase them down after they hurt people."

Arthur glanced over and saw that Desiree wasn't even looking at him. He watched the realization of what he had said sink in. How hard, he wondered, must this be to hear?

"Leopold...he's been such a huge part of my life...I've never really thought about what things would be like if he was gone."

"I know what you mean. I felt the same way about my family. I took them for granted. For the first several days after they were gone I couldn't even come to terms with the idea of them being dead, and for months after I didn't know what I was supposed to be without them. I'm still not sure what I'm supposed to do now that they are gone. I mean, what is the right thing?"

"Maybe exactly what you are doing?" she said. A moment passed in silence. Suddenly she burst out laughing. "Well, you know, minus the kidnapping people part."

He chuckled. "I really am sorry about that."

"I get it. I mean, I don't get it, but I forgive you for

it. You aren't really the trusting sort, are you?"

"Not anymore."

They stood in the entrance to his cabin for a moment longer. Arthur needed to go gather up his supplies and get back on the road, but he felt awkward just walking away. He cleared his throat.

"Well, uh...I better—"

"What do I do now?" she interrupted. Her expression turned back to pensive, her mood somber.

"What do you mean?"

"I mean, what am I supposed to do next with my life? How do I move on from this?"

"That's up to you. Now that Leopold is out of your way you can do anything you want. Are you ready to leave this cabin and get back out into the real world?"

"Go back home, you mean?"

She acted like the idea was a terrible one. Arthur frowned. "Yeah. The Bishop is gone and you shouldn't have anything else to worry about. You can return to your life. Just tell the people you know that you took a short sabbatical, sorted things out, and things can just go back to normal."

She hesitated. "What is normal? Normal for me has been keeping to myself and dreading waking up every morning for fear of what Leopold might do to me. I honestly don't know if I have a life to go back to."

"What do you mean?"

"I spent the last thirty years being afraid of Leopold and what he could do to me. I never really had a chance to stop and evaluate my situation, you know? I just kept on running, going through the motions, and always glancing back over my shoulder. I ... don't really think I want to go home. Not yet, at least. There's nothing to go back home to."

Arthur knew what she meant. It was the same thing he'd been dealing with himself since his family had died. The farmhouse where he grew up and raised his daughter felt like a foreign place now, a part of another life that was no longer his.

"So, where do you want to go instead?" he asked. "You can take Niccolo's car and go anywhere. I'll pay for the rental as long as you need it."

She shrugged. "I don't know where to start. You tell me I can go anywhere, but instead of too many options it feels like I have none. I want to … I don't know. I want for my life to have meaning. I want it to be more than just this. Where are you guys going?"

"Ohio."

"Can I come with you?"

"No."

"Why not?"

Arthur laughed, shaking his head. "You can't go with us."

She frowned, and Arthur realized she wasn't joking. She was dead serious. "Why not?"

"Where we're going, it'll be dangerous, and you aren't exactly ready for something like that."

"I've been practicing with that silly dart gun you left me for the last couple of days. I can hit the bullseye pretty often now. I'm also a trained lawyer and great at research. I'm sure that could come in handy, wouldn't it?"

"That's a stretch."

"Still."

"You aren't ready for something like this. It'll be risky and we don't know what we are up against."

"What about Niccolo? He wasn't ready and you still took him out there."

"And look what that got him? He won't talk and killed a man. Clearly, I made the wrong call."

It was a sore spot for Arthur: he knew that what had happened to Niccolo was as much his fault as the priest's, if not more. He never should have brought Niccolo along in the first place. When he went out after the Bishop, he should have gone alone, no matter how insistent the priest was that he could handle it.

The truth of the matter was: this wasn't Niccolo's world. He had lived a sheltered life, protected from the dangerous underbelly of Arthur's world.

Niccolo could help when it came to church matters and exorcisms, but he wasn't ready for something like this. Arthur had been so caught up in what use he could get out of Niccolo he hadn't stopped to think that maybe it would end up hurting him.

Arthur should have known better.

"I'm not him, though." Desiree said.

"No, you're not Niccolo, but you also aren't a Hunter. The things we do are dangerous. More importantly, though, you don't deserve to have to deal with something like this. With the Bishop gone, you've been given a clean slate and a chance to start over. Don't waste it."

"I'm not wasting it. It's my slate, and I want to help. I don't need to go anywhere dangerous with you. If you think a situation will be risky, then you can just leave me behind. Just let me come along, though. I can help, or I can stay out of your way, but right now I only know two things for certain: I can't go back home, and I sure as hell don't want to stay here. No offense."

"None taken."

"So, can I come with you?"

Arthur thought it over. He had no intention of

bringing her – or Niccolo, for that matter – into any situation that might end up being difficult or dangerous, but he could sympathize with her desire to stay busy. It was the same thing he was trying to do with Niccolo.

If nothing else, he could get her out of Colorado until she decided she was ready to go home. Plus, the selfish side of Arthur knew having her along would help with a lot of logistics: it meant one more driver to keep them moving until they reached Ohio.

"If I say yes, you will do whatever I say when I say it, right?"

"Of course. You tell me to jump, I'll just ask how high. You're the boss."

He laughed. "First time anyone's ever called me that."

"So, we have a deal?"

"Yeah," he said. "Ever been to Ohio this time of year?"

"No, why?"

"It's going to be cold. Don't worry, we'll pick up some coats on the way. Let's finish packing and get on the road. We've got a long way to go."

***

They made good time on their cross-country trek from Colorado to Ohio. He got them well on the way until about two in the morning, at which point she took over while he got some rest.

A few times either Desiree or Arthur tried striking up a conversation with him, but Niccolo didn't even acknowledge their questions. Finally, Desiree gave up and spoke only to Arthur.

He had to admit, having her on the road was a pleasant distraction from just riding with Niccolo. She was talkative and interesting to listen to, telling stories about her life, family, and road trips she had taken when she was young. She was also quite funny and intelligent.

"So, what is our plan when we get there?" Desiree asked when they were about halfway to Ohio. They had just gotten back on the road after a fast food stop and driver change, and Arthur was lying out in the back seat with his eyes closed.

He hadn't managed to actually fall asleep, though. He was too busy worrying over that exact question. He honestly didn't know what to expect or where to start searching for Jeremy. He had a couple of ideas of people he could ask, and he knew how important it would be to find Jeremy quickly. He knew how dangerous the child was and the kind of damage he could cause if left to his own devices.

"I don't know," he admitted. "I don't have the slightest inkling what Jeremy is planning or where to start looking. If you've got any ideas, I'm open to suggestions."

"I wish I did. If only I had access to the Bishop's paperwork."

"The Church has their best people looking through them as we speak."

"The church's best people?" she asked skeptically. "Will they tell us if they find anything?"

"I hope so," Arthur admitted. He could understand her lack of trust for the Church, though. He didn't have a lot of faith either.

"At least he's only a child," she said. "And the Bishop is out of the picture. What kind of damage can he really do alone like this?"

"You have no idea."

"What do you mean?"

"He was the central piece of the Bishop's plan to build his army in Everett."

"Really?"

"It gets worse. When I was back at the shipyard, he got into my head."

"Into your head?"

"Like controlling my thoughts. Forcing suggestions for me to do things, and it almost worked."

"How the hell can he do something like that?"

"No clue. He's psychic, and it was like he was ... suppressing me. Like he was taking over my mind and pushing me down. It was almost like demonic possession."

"Demons are real, too?"

Arthur laughed. "You've got a lot to catch up on."

"I guess so. Was he able to read your thoughts?"

"I don't know. All I know is that he was able to suppress my thoughts, at least for a few seconds, and make me vulnerable. I'm not sure how I'm supposed to deal with that when I face him."

"Your dart gun works pretty well."

"Yeah. If I can get a shot off. The thing is, no matter what happens I need to get the jump on him. Not the other way around. If he sees me coming I won't stand a chance."

"Where are we going to start looking?"

"You," he said, emphasizing the word, "are going to lay low and wait until we hear back from the Church or something changes. If nothing happens, then I'm going to search around, talk to people I know, and try to shake something loose."

"If you don't have a lead, why are we in such a hurry?"

"I'm guessing Jeremy is going to be impatient and want things to happen quickly, so I don't think we'll be lacking a lead for very long."

"Maybe I can be of assistance outside of knocking on doors with you."

"What do you mean?"

"Well, I told you I'm good at researching things. Local news and whatnot. I had to do it a lot for the law firm I interned at to find clients. I'll go to a local library and see if I can find something that might indicate a target Jeremy would pick."

"You think that will work?"

"Beats me, but if the Bishop had this place pegged as his biggest target, then he's probably got some history here. If we can figure out what that is, we'll have the upper hand."

Arthur shrugged. It was worth a shot. "Let's hope so."

Chapter 2

"We're here."

The booming voice of the driver woke Jeremy up from his slumber with a jolt. He found himself blinking and groggy in the backseat of the black Ford SUV he'd spent the last three days cooped up in. He was disoriented and confused: it took him a minute to remember his journey and mission.

Or his father's recent death.

The pangs of loss hit him like a punch in the stomach, taking his breath away. His heart ached and he doubted it would ever stop hurting. He'd spent the better part of the trip crying and wallowing in self-pity over the loss of Bishop Glasser.

Empty fast food wrappers surrounded him in the backseat like a disgusting fort and it smelled musty and rotten. He hated every single moment he had spent in this vehicle traveling to Ohio.

"We're here," the driver repeated, looking at him in the mirror.

"I heard you the first time," he said, grabbing a half empty drink from a cup holder. His mouth tasted horrible, like cotton. He took a sip of the diluted beverage and let out a groan. "I'm not deaf."

"My apologies, sir."

The driver was the last remnant of what he had from the previous mission out in California. He had been guarding Jeremy while they were at that shipyard, and he had dragged Jeremy away after the Bishop was killed.

He followed orders well enough. Fighting, though...not so much. A bottom tier demon in a less than exceptional vessel. The last demon they had summoned before Leopold died, before he was brutally murdered by that sycophantic priest.

Jeremy hadn't wanted to flee the docks, nor leave his father, but he knew the hunter was the real danger. He'd heard stories about Arthur Vangeest from the Bishop, and he knew better than to stand in his way.

Demon Hunters: a festering rot as far as Jeremy was concerned. He would have killed him just to rid the world of another of his kind. They murdered and butchered everyone, working outside the law. Still, fighting him was problematic: it wasn't a fight he would willing to engage in while he didn't have to.

Jeremy yawned and stretched a little bit, rolling down the window. He didn't recognize the scenery, and they weren't at a restaurant.

"Where is here, exactly?"

"Akron, Ohio. We're at the location you requested. Megyn Willford's hideout."

Jeremy perked up a little bit. He hadn't realized he'd slept for as long as he did and they were already at their final destination. Megyn's home away from home. However, when he glanced out the window at the service station again, he saw a worn and abandoned building off an old country road.

It didn't even connect back to a major highway for twenty miles. The building was collapsing in on itself and seemed at least thirty years old.

"This is the place?" he asked skeptically. It didn't look livable at all.

"Yes."

"You're sure?"

"Quite."

Jeremy shrugged. Megyn had been living here for

months, hiding away until the time came for the events to begin. She had three loyalists staying with her, caring for her and protecting her from discovery. Jeremy had known them for years, back when he and Megyn were training together with the Bishop.

Jeremy, not Megyn, had been the one to accompany the Bishop to Everett. He had been the favorite, not her.

Bishop Glasser had recruited dozens of people to his cause over the last forty years, but most of them were just normal civilians who believed he did important work. They followed him, but offered little except for their sycophantic devotion.

Useless servants, in point of fact.

Jeremy groaned at the idea of living in the service station. He had spent the last few months living a life of opulence with the Bishop in Everett. This simply would not do.

At least they wouldn't have to be here for long.

"This dump is the best we can do? There are no other hideaways or safe houses in the area?"

"I don't know, sir."

"How can you expect me to live here even if only for a few days?"

"I don't know, sir."

Jeremy waved his hand in the air. It was a rhetorical question, but sometimes this particular demon was too stupid to understand conversational nuances.

Of course this was the best they could do right now. Anything more elaborate ran the risk of discovery, and even as important as Megyn was to the cause she wasn't worth more resources wasted on her.

"Alright. Come on, let's go."

Jeremy opened the door and stepped out of the car, and the demon moved to follow. They headed across the cracked pavement of the street to the dingy service station that would serve as his home for the next couple of days.

He just had to hope that the inside was better than the outside.

***

The door opened before he could knock on it and he saw a woman standing just inside. She had a pistol in her hand, but for now it was hanging down at her side instead of aiming at him.

She looked to be in her mid-fifties, though Jeremy knew from experience that she was actually much younger. A rat face and beady eyes. Bishop Glasser had assured him in the past that she was once quite a beautiful young woman, but Jeremy didn't believe him. Leathery and awful skin adorned her face and she smelled rancid.

He had requested that Leopold send her with Megyn so many months ago simply so he wouldn't have to see her anymore. She had a soft spot for him, though, and he knew just what buttons to press to get his way.

"Come now, Aunt Sheila. Is that anyway to greet your favorite nephew?"

A moment passed, and then her eyes went wide. "Jeremy?"

"The one and only," he said, smiling at her. "Aren't you going to give me a hug?"

She slipped the gun back into the waist of her pants and rushed out the door to him. She squeezed him tightly, and he squeezed back, careful not to breathe during the embrace. It was quite a bit worse than normal: she smelled like she hadn't showered in weeks, but it might have been months.

"What are you doing here?" she asked breathlessly once they had separated. "Aren't you supposed to be in India by now?"

"That was the plan," he said. "Things have changed though and we have new business to attend to. I'd rather not talk about it out here. Is there somewhere inside we can talk?"

"Certainly. Megyn will be thrilled to see you."

He doubted it. "I can't wait," he lied. "I've been dying to see my sister for months."

Of course, Megyn wasn't his real sister any more than Leopold had been their real father. Nor was Sheila his real aunt. Leopold was the one who formed them into a family. His mission became their reality. He offered them a way forward and had been the anchor point of their extended family.

Without him, the family was on the verge of disintegration. Jeremy had to hold them together at least a little while longer.

Just thinking about that moment on the docks when Bishop Glasser had been shot in the face caused Jeremy's fists to clench. He needed to hold his family together until they had gotten revenge. He'd never been so angry and frustrated about anything in his entire life.

The Bishop's vision had been left unrealized with his death, but as long as Jeremy lived, the plan would continue. It would, in fact, evolve and become even stronger. Jeremy would find a way to finish what Leopold Glasser had started back in Everett.

"Have your driver pull the car out back," Sheila said. "There's a little shed he can park in so he's off the road and out of sight. We've boarded up the windows and locked the place down so we don't want to draw any attention."

Jeremy turned and nodded to the driver, letting him know it was alright to follow Sheila's order. Then he followed Sheila into the service station. Even with how disgusting and rundown the place was, he was glad to be here because it meant realizing the beginning of the mission he'd set for himself after the Bishop died.

He had chosen this location to begin his attack for a couple of reasons. After all, there were children stationed all around the country he could have joined, but Megyn had been the one in the most important location in Southeastern Ohio. She was also one of the most powerful children of the bunch, and on top of that this place was targeted specifically to get vengeance for crimes committed against Bishop Glasser.

Leopold had warned against putting two powerful children so close together. They would create a target that could be easily stopped by the Church and its allies. However, Jeremy had thought of the perfect solution to that exact problem: he would use the other children as bait.

He had sent activation messages to all of the other cells with the special children. Many of them were unprepared for such an uprising and would be unsuccessful in their missions, but that mattered little. Some would probably die, but they were acceptable losses given the greater mission that was at stake. They had known the risks when they were recruited and trained by the Bishop.

They would form the perfect distractions, however,

to give him time to finalize his plan. All Jeremy needed to do was keep the Church busy while he embarked on the attack that would make the Bishop proud. He would garner international attention, he knew, and redeem his father.

***

They walked deeper into the grimy service station, pushing a swing door open and moving into the dimly lit storage room. His mind's eye showed a thriving gas station long ago, but now it was just a building waiting for a demolition crew.

"Megyn," Sheila said softly, holding up her hand to warn Jeremy to stop moving. "You can come out now, honey."

Jeremy heard the familiar click of a pistol cocking from off to his left, and he froze in place. His eyes hadn't adjusted to the darkness yet so he couldn't see anything more than a shape.

"Who is he? You! Don't take another step."

"I didn't intend to take one. Megyn, is that you?"

A hesitation. "Jeremy?"

"Yes. It's me."

Three people walked out of the darkness. One man, a second older woman, and then a girl about twelve years old. The man he didn't recognize: he was balding with a flannel shirt on and missing teeth. He carried a shotgun.

The woman was in her twenties, probably, with bug eyes and an unpleasant face. Jeremy didn't know her by name, but he had met her at some point in the past. She looked familiar.

The little girl was Megyn Wilford. She was a pretty little thirteen year old girl with flowing blonde hair and a big smile. She was also the most powerful telekinetic child of the group, able to do things that had impressed even him.

"Why are you here?" the bug-eyed woman asked. She demanded it of him, and Jeremy was annoyed. "What is going on? Where is Leopold?"

"There's been a change in plans."

"What do you mean?"

He hated answering this woman's questions. Who the hell did she think she was? She was a normal civilian, not special like him or Megyn. He didn't owe her any explanation; right now he wanted nothing more than to lash out at her mentality and force her to grovel at his feet.

He needed to use tact, however, to win Megyn over. To bring his plan to fruition he would need for Megyn to trust him, which meant being diplomatic.

"I mean it is time for us to get to work. Lower your gun and let's all talk. We have much to discuss."

***

"I want to talk to him," Megyn said. Jeremy had finished explaining the situation to her (at least, the modified situation he had concocted to get her help). She had listened patiently, growing more anxious as Jeremy spoke. She wrung her hands and scowled at him.

His version of events didn't contain the Bishop's murder. That fact he conveniently left out.

"I told you, he is very busy."

"I can call him. He told me I could call him whenever I needed him."

"He is off the radar since the Church is looking for him. If you call him now you will be putting him at risk. But he sent me here to put things into motion and we have a lot to do."

"Father was very specific that we had to wait for him to activate us. Not you, Jeremy."

Jeremy waved his hand in annoyance. He felt like they had been having the same circular conversation for the last hour with no progress. It was starting to frustrate him. Megyn was persistent about that one sticking issue, and he knew she was right: Leopold had made it abundantly clear that they were only to listen to him.

Jeremy couldn't very well conjure up the Bishop to talk to her, though. Sending the messages to other children hadn't been very difficult: they were waiting for coded messages anyway, and impersonating the Bishop wasn't difficult like that. In person, though, things were trickier.

He considered admitting that their Father was dead. It was a fine line to not tell Megyn the full truth, but he couldn't risk compromising his agenda by her having a breakdown because of her tender emotions.

She couldn't know of the murder of her father. If she found out then she would never agree to his plan.

"I know, Megyn."

"It just seems like a major divergence from our original objective."

"You know me. Would I lie about something like this?"

She hesitated, and for a minute he worried that she might say 'yes.' Finally, she shook her head.

"No, of course not. It just seems odd that he didn't contact me to tell me you were coming."

"I told you: the Church was on to his plans and they are chasing him, so he had to speed up our timetable. He was afraid to make any calls or contact until he could evade the church, but by then we need to have acted. We are supposed to distract them to give him a chance to escape."

"OK."

"We are out of time, though, so we need to handle this as quickly as possible."

She started to open her mouth to speak and then changed her mind. Finally, she said, "Ok. So, what do we do?"

"In due time," Jeremy said. "First, though, how long has it been since you got to eat ice cream?"

He could tell from the sudden grin on her face that his guess had been right: it had been a long time. He fished some money out of his pocket. He didn't have much left, but this was important.

"I saw a shop about a mile up the road. How about you go get yourself a scoop and bring it back?"

"Sure," she said, accepted the offered money. She turned to the other adults in the room, settling on Sheila. "Are you guys coming?"

"They are going to hang out here with me," Jeremy cut in before Sheila could respond. "We have a lot of things to get ready for the Bishop's plan to work, and we'll be ready to go by the time you get back."

"Ok," Megyn said. Humming to herself, she walked across the room and back into the main area of the service station.

Jeremy turned to the demon driver he'd brought with him. "Is the car stowed?"

"Yes."

"Why did you send her off?" Sheila asked.

To her credit, there was a slight waver in her tone. Jeremy didn't answer her question, but turned his attention instead to the man holding the shotgun. He reached out mentally, testing his fortitude. A weak willed man, he determined, easily dominated.

Jeremy gave him the suggestion to aim the gun at Sheila. "Put your gun down, Aunty," he said, smiling pleasantly at Sheila.

"What are you doing?"

"I won't ask you again. Please set your pistol on the floor."

"Jeremy...what are you doing? What's going on?"

"I don't much like the idea of you second guessing me, and I don't need any of you."

Her lip quivered. "You won't have him shoot me. Megyn would hear."

"I'd rather not have anyone get shot," Jeremy replied. "It would spoil the organs."

Sheila's eyes went wide. "You intend to harvest us."

"It wasn't my original plan, but then she started second guessing me," he said, pointing at the younger woman. "And the thing is, I don't like having people question me. If there was any other way..."

The bug eyed woman turned and ran for the door. Jeremy mentally overpowered her and forced her to fall to her knees. She groveled there, and he felt a smile spreading across his face.

"Much better."

"Jeremy, you don't have to do this."

"I know. Obviously I don't have to. But, for what I have planned I'm going to need a lot of organs, and I'd rather get as many of them as I can before letting anyone know I'm here."

"We've served Leopold faithfully for years. If he has any idea what you are—"

"Leopold is dead," he said flatly. "Go figure. Guess that means he won't care much what I do with you."

The shotgun shook, the man struggling to break free of Jeremy's grip on his mind. "Start with him," he said, nodding for his bodyguard to begin. "And be careful not to damage any of the precious bits."

"Jeremy—"

"I think you're done," he said, turning to look at Sheila. He seized her, stopping her from speaking. She was a lot stronger than the man, nearly breaking free of his mental grip, but he held her grip.

Jeremy watched as his driver moved from one to the next, slicing their throats. He overpowered them, and forced them into submission, unable to get free. As the blood drained out, so did the light from their eyes.

The smell of their coppery blood was overpowering as it pooled across the dusty floor and he walked back to make sure it didn't get on his feet.

"Hurry up and get what we need into the cooler. I'll stop Megyn outside and we'll be in the car waiting for you. I'd rather not have her see any of this."

"Understood."

"Make it look like there was a struggle. Make it look like the Hunter killed them."

"Why?

He smiled. "Every story needs a good villain. Once Megyn sees what they did to her friends, she'll have no choice but to help me."

He turned and strode back out of the service station with a sigh. It was an unpleasantly hot day, and he was starting to wish he'd asked Megyn to pick him up some ice cream, too.

Chapter 3

Arthur was still a little unsure of his decision to bring Desiree along with them all the way to Ohio. Her driving helped, but he had no idea what sort of danger they were heading into. It wouldn't be fair or right to bring her out of one dangerous situation and into another one.

It had been her decision, though, and it would have been even less fair to refuse her help simply out of his own pride. In the end, it was better to have three heads instead of two in trying to figure out what was going on in Ohio with Jeremy ... especially since one of those heads was still being quiet and withdrawn.

Niccolo barely spoke, but his animation increased dramatically. He was out of his own thoughts at least a little bit. Even still, for most of the drive the tension in the car felt thick enough to cut with a knife.

The priest would answer questions and offer up suggestions occasionally, but when he was in one of his moods at least Arthur could converse with Desiree and stay occupied.

It was a long couple of days driving to reach Athens, Ohio, but once he was finally there Arthur's first plan was to reach out to his brother for help, hoping to get a seedier picture of the city and what they were up against.

He chose Athens because he knew the territory very well. Just to the northeast of Columbus and a quick shot to any heavily trafficked places Jeremy might hit. It could serve as an initial base of operations for them while they tried to figure out what Jeremy was planning.

If he was being honest, however, he also picked the

city of Athens because it was close to his home.

He spent a sizable chunk of his youth near Amish Country and it was a familiar place. Being back here was simultaneously relaxing and painful: this was also the city where he'd lost his family.

He paused at an intersection in downtown Athens, however. Turning right would take them to the hotel, but even as the light shifted to green he just let the car idle.

A minute passed. The light changed back to red.

"What's going on?" Desiree asked, leaning up from the backseat. "Do you need the map?"

"No," he said, rubbing his face with his hands. Behind them, a car started honking as the light changed back to green once more. His turn signal kept blinking at him and he felt sweat beading on his forehead.

"You said we were almost to the hotel, right?"

"Yeah," he said. "We are. That's not where we are going, though."

He flipped the turn signal to turn left instead. He had made up his mind about something he needed to do now that he was back in his old stomping grounds, and it was better to get it taken care of early than to drag it out.

"Where are we going, then?"

Arthur didn't immediately answer. This was something he had put off for the last several months, a trip he needed to make.

"Home."

✳✳✳

"Where are we?" Niccolo asked as Arthur turned off the paved road and onto a gravel drive. The car jostled a little bit and kicked up a cloud of dust behind them as they went. He looked around, groggy, and turned to Arthur. "Are we almost to the hotel?"

Arthur didn't immediately reply: his palms were sweaty and the air felt hot around him. He tugged at his collar, finding it suddenly difficult to breathe. Even his knuckles turned white as they gripped the steering wheel and he forced them to relax. He felt Desiree's hand on his shoulder. She must have sensed his discomfort.

The way the gravel crunched under the tires was something Arthur had heard a thousand times before. A million, even. It was a comforting sound, but also jarring in the memories it elicited. How many times had he come this way with his daughter in the backseat, her laughter filling the car?

He brushed the sweat off of his forehead and took several deep and steadying breaths.

"I thought we were going to the hotel?" Niccolo said, seeing the house looming up ahead.

"We still might," Arthur replied. "I just need to make a quick stop, first."

Niccolo was quiet for a moment. "This is your home, isn't it?"

Arthur didn't answer. He could see the town house in the distance, next to the old red barn and paddock. He'd painted that house about a year ago, giving it a fresh coat that shined in the waning sunlight.

Both the barn and the fields were empty now and forgotten, the horses long since sold off.

Mitchell oversaw the farm while Arthur struggled to find his way back. While Arthur had been too broken to actually deal with the world around him and wanted nothing more than to just crawl into a hole and die, Mitchell took care of the property for him. He never really said so aloud, but he was thankful for his brother and knew that by now he would have lost the house—or worse—if not for him.

He didn't blame Mitchell for that, though. It had been his own fault for trusting the Council to protect them. He should have kept his family better hidden, more secret.

Or, better yet, he should have taken his brother's advice and never gotten married in the first place. He had known the risks when he first met his future wife and eventually had his beautiful daughter, though it was something he'd never believed could happen. Not to him.

He'd been too foolish to actually believe in the possibility that he might lose everything.

Still, he didn't regret it ... not fully, at least. After everything that had happened, he knew it was better to have tried to be happy than to resign himself without ever making the effort.

"This is your home?" Desiree asked as he parked in front of the front porch. The drive ended at a large circular parking area big enough to fit about eight vehicles.

"This was my home," he corrected. "Not anymore, though. Now it is just a property I own. We can stay here for the next couple of days and save the hotel cost."

"Are you sure?" Niccolo asked. "I can pay for the hotel if need be and –"

"I'm sure," Arthur said. Not an ideal time for such a trip, but he knew that the longer he put it off, the more difficult it would become.

The time was now.

Still, he made no immediate move to exit the car, just kept taking deep breaths and willing for the emotions to subside. His mind kept wandering to memories of his family and life before.

No one spoke for another few minutes while Arthur continued staring at the front door of his country home. He couldn't see anything in his mind except for the blood of his family on the kitchen floor. The looks on their faces.

"Could you maybe give us a tour?"

The question came from Desiree, and it jolted him back out of his memories. He realized that a long while must have passed in his reverie, and he shook his head to clear the thoughts away.

He tried to focus on something else, willing forth good memories of his life spent here. It wasn't all bad, he knew, and it wouldn't be fair to let the bad outweigh the good. He'd been raised here, played with his brother in the fields, worked with his father in the barn.

When his parents had died they'd still been just teenagers. Without a will, the house had been left to both of them to share. Neither of them knew what to do about that; Mitchell had eventually forfeited his claim to Arthur years later as a wedding present when he'd just turned twenty.

He did it, he said, so that Arthur could raise his family here, and it had been the happiest day of his life. This home was full of good memories.

But it was also full of death.

"Sure. A tour sounds like a great idea. Let's start with the barn," he said finally.

He brushed angrily at his wet cheeks and opened

the car door. They all stepped out into the sunshine. The air felt good on his skin and it was nice being able to stretch his legs.

The other two followed him as he walked across the gravel driveway to the old red barn. He'd spent a lot of time out there, playing hide and seek with his brother or grooming the horses. His father had worked at a nearby racetrack taking care of dozens of race horses and they stabled quite a few of the animals during the long and cold winters.

He'd loved riding around the fields, though he hadn't gotten to do it more than a handful of times with his father. The man spent his hours working and never gave Arthur his time. There was something peaceful about just running around the fields and spending a few hours enjoying the sunshine and wind.

After his parents died so suddenly the place fell into modest disrepair. Neither he nor his brother really knew how to take care of a family home this big, but when he'd married his wife he'd fixed the place back up. He'd even rebuilt the barn to start stabling horses again.

It was as though he'd gotten a new lease on life. He wanted his daughter to experience riding horses around the fields the way he had with his parents. He wanted to share this part of his childhood with his daughter. He'd always just put it off.

Now she was gone.

Now he would never have the chance.

The guilt of it all weighed heavily on him as he slid open the old barn door. The rusty railing needed oil. The smell of hay and wood assaulted his senses as he stepped inside, moving out of the sunlight and into the shadowy interior of the barn.

Sunlight flitted in from overhead through cracks in the ceiling and walls, and he could see dust hanging in the air around them in little streams of light.

The hay loft overhead was starting to sag and one of the beams had almost completely rotted away. Termites would tear the place down eventually, but he wasn't sure if he even cared. He knew he should spend some time treating the wood and fixing the barn back up, but he doubted he ever would.

He had good memories of being in the barn, but it felt like another life. Another person, not him, had enjoyed spending time out here. That man was dead.

"This was where we raised horses," he said flatly, gesturing at the barn around him. "When I was little, every stall was full and we would spend about five hours a day out here working."

"Working?"

"Yep," Arthur said. "Takes a lot of time to groom and feed the animals. At least, if you want to do it right; that was my childhood."

"Did you raise baby horses?" Desiree asked.

He nodded. "We had foals occasionally, depending on which owner my father was working for at the time. All of that ended when I was fifteen, though, so it's been a long time. I would ride the horses around the field when I wasn't supposed to and then would spend long hours out there searching for the lost horseshoes because of it. My father was a blacksmith and he would chide me before tacking them back on."

"Sounds fun."

"It was. My brother didn't join me very often. He didn't much care for the horses and would avoid them at all costs, but with my father there weren't a lot of options. He was a strict man. He died when I was a teenager."

"I'm sorry."

Arthur shrugged. "It is what it is."

He turned away and headed back outside of the barn. He bypassed the empty paddock; the only place left: the house. He knew that going in there wouldn't be as easy of a reunion, but he started walking that way just the same. One foot in front of the other. He heard Desiree and Niccolo trailing behind.

He knew the interior of the house would be clean. There wouldn't see any traces of the violence that had taken place there. Mitchell had long since fixed it up, hiring a professional cleaning crew that worked for the police to make sure no traces were left.

That almost made it worse, though. It was as though his wife and daughter had been scrubbed out of existence.

"Mitchell has been taking care of the place for the last several months," he explained, more to distract himself than for his guests. Talking helped occupy his mind. "He's been a real life saver, but he lives several hours away so the place has been unoccupied. I offered to give the house back to him after my family was killed, but he wasn't interested. I think he thinks I'll move back in at some point, but I have no intention of doing that because there is no way I'm going to live where—"

His phone started buzzing. Arthur jerked in surprise and stumbled to the side.

He glanced at Desiree and Niccolo, both of whom had solemn and serious expressions on their faces. Both of them, however, stifled laughter at his reaction.

The image was so ridiculous that he burst out laughing. He slid the phone out of his pocket and glanced at the name on the little screen. Frieda. He flipped the phone open and held it to his ear.

"Yeah, Frieda?"

"Saint Thomas Church," she said without any preamble. "Get there."

"On our way," he said. "What are we expecting—?"

He heard a click on the other end as Frieda hung up.

"Never mind," he said, putting the phone back in his pocket.

She was probably in a hurry to do something, though he would have liked a little more information about what they were going to find out at the church.

He knew where it was: it was south of here, somewhere outside of Akron, a little less than an hour away. He turned and headed back toward the car.

"Come on," he said. "Time to go."

"Is it a lead?"

"Should be."

He had to admit a flood of relief that he didn't have to go into the actual house. Not yet at least. It was nice having at least a temporary reprieve from that emotional confrontation.

"Where are we going?" Niccolo asked, heading around to the passenger seat.

"A nearby Church, about an hour away."

"Do you mind if I stay here?" Desiree asked suddenly. "My stomach has been queasy from the last couple of days driving and I would love a chance to lie down for a bit."

"Sure."

Arthur headed over to unlock the front door of the house for her. His hand shook as he walked up the front steps.

"The bedrooms should all be unlocked, though

things might be a little dusty. I don't think my brother has been here in months."

"I'll probably just lie down the couch."

"Make yourself at home," he said, unlocking the door before rushing back down the steps. His heart raced from being so close to where they died and he didn't dare look back. "We should be back soon."

Once he was safely inside the car, he flipped the ignition on and peeled off down the driveway back to the main road. He knew the Church from his childhood: a place he had attended for a short while when he was about eight. Catholic parents, but not religious. His mother, in particular, wasn't much for church.

They had attended a few times in his life, but never longer than a month or two at a time. It was just a fight his father wasn't willing to have.

"Was it one of the children?" Niccolo asked as they drove. "Was there an attack? Is Jeremy involved?"

"I don't know yet," Arthur replied. He tried dialing Frieda again, but she didn't answer. "Most likely."

They continued in silence for a while before Niccolo finally spoke again.

"It must have been difficult. Being back there."

Arthur hesitated. "It wasn't what I expected."

"What do you mean?"

"It was painful, but it was terrifying in a completely different way. It felt like reopening a wound, something I had already dealt with."

"You never fully close a wound like that," Niccolo agreed. "Still, it's important that you face it."

"I know," Arthur replied. "It was just … different."

Part of him worried that he might find closure for this chapter of his life. Would that be unfair to the wife and daughter he had lost? The family that died because of him?

He didn't know.

What he did know was that he needed to find closure. He had chosen to adopt Abigail as his daughter after he rescued her from that cult. He would take care of her, and for that to happen he needed to find a way to come to peace with everything that had happened before. He couldn't remain the split and unfocused man he'd been for these last months.

Abigail didn't deserve that.

First things first, though. Whatever the Bishop had planned, a lot of people would die. He couldn't allow his emotions to cloud his judgment.

Chapter 4
Three Hours Earlier

"Where are we going?"

"You ask a lot of questions," Jeremy said, growing more and more frustrated by the minute as they rode in the back of the SUV. Megyn wouldn't quit her incessant whining and it was grating on his nerves. It had taken him ten minutes of begging and prodding just to get her into the car, and he'd thought he won the battle at that point.

Truth be told, it had taken a lot longer for his driver to harvest the organs than anticipated, and Megyn didn't like just sitting in the car waiting with him. She wanted an explanation that he wasn't willing or able to give. He couldn't very well let her walk back into the service station, though, so he just lied.

The other three of her friends would meet them there, he explained. They were out gathering supplies for the mission and everything was completely normal. He had never guessed it would be so difficult to convince Megyn that they were on a timetable and needed to get this done fast.

Finally, the demon driver had returned and gotten them on the way, but even now Megyn wouldn't stop questioning him.

"I ask a lot of questions because I want to know where you're taking me," Megyn said, sounding very motherly.

"It's a very important mission," he explained. "I promise you that everything will be made clear when we get there. We should arrive in the next couple of minutes."

"Will our Father meet us there?"

"No. I told you, he's out of the country right now. We are doing this for him, however. He will be very proud of us."

She sighed. "Fine."

He bit back his annoyance and turned to look ahead of the car instead. He wanted to slap some sense into her so she would stop asking about the Bishop. It was painful enough for Jeremy just having to think about the man, let alone worry about constantly lying to her that Leopold was still alive.

They drove toward a church on the outskirts of Akron, hard to reach and secluded. That's what made it the perfect target: no one would know anything was happening until it was too late. It was also Saturday, which meant there would be some people at the church, but not more than they could handle.

"When are we going to see him?"

"Soon. When he gets back to the States this is going to be the first place he comes. I promise."

She didn't like that answer, but Jeremy didn't much care. He didn't have time to worry about her emotions or insecurities: he had a job to do, and that was honoring Leopold's legacy.

That meant punishing the Bishop's enemies.

✳✳✳

He had been a lowly priest living in Akron, Ohio. He had ministered at a little Church out in the country. The Church of Saint Thomas. His small and devout flock turned out to be monstrous people. They had turned against him and made up lies and rumors to harm his reputation, calling him a child molester and worse. He was run out of town, seeking haven in another city to the south in Alabama to lick his wounds and regroup.

He hadn't forgotten, though: that church and those people were why Megyn was stationed here. Her duty was to earn the vengeance he'd never been able to find. He wanted for those people to pay for their crimes against him, to suffer as he'd suffered.

Leopold had confided this secret to Jeremy, never telling the other children about his secret failing in Ohio. He had trusted Jeremy would keep the information to himself until the time was right.

That time was now.

If Jeremy was being honest, he had always been a little bit offended that Leopold stationed Megyn here and not him. Something this important shouldn't be left up to a little girl, no matter how powerful.

No doubt it was because he wanted to keep Jeremy close to his side, though. That was the only reason that made sense. Jeremy was Leopold's second in command, and the Bishop wouldn't risk his safety just to pay back his betrayers.

"That's it, up ahead," he said, spotting the church in the distance.

It was a little white building sitting atop on a hill and surrounded by barren trees. The nearest house was over a half-mile away and it was impossible to see very far through the thick woods in all directions.

The perfect place to launch his mission.

This would be his crowning victory, punishing the people who had tried to harm the Bishop's reputation so long ago. Thankfully, the Church had sided with him against the town's lies. He was simply stationed in other cities and throughout Europe until the furor died down.

He'd since presided over many churches, schools, and other Catholic organizations in his time as a priest, but this was the one that damaged him the most. This was his first.

"Park just around the corner. You'll wait in the car until we need you."

"Yes sir."

The driver pulled the car into the lot and into one of the empty spots. There were plenty of them. He kept the engine on and glanced at Jeremy in the backseat.

Jeremy didn't have to worry about his loyalty. The demon might be a little slow but he was also willing to do anything Jeremy asked of him. He had loved the Bishop as a father the same as Jeremy. He too wanted vengeance.

Jeremy nodded at him in the mirror. He understood the full ramifications of what they were trying to accomplish here and how important it was. If Megyn refused to join them …

He took a calming breath and pushed the concern away. No time for such thoughts. There was only one path: forward.

He climbed out of the car and into the midday sunlight. He held the door for Megyn and beckoned for her to follow.

"Come on."

"It's so cold."

"I know," he said, pulling his coat tighter. It had dropped at least twenty degrees since they first started driving. The volatility of the weather annoyed him. It hadn't been cold in California, but winter's here were much less comfortable. "We're going inside, though, so it'll be alright."

Hesitantly, she slid across the seat and stood up. She looked at the wide building with a concerned expression on her face.

"Why are we here?"

"All will be revealed, sister. Follow me."

He didn't wait for her response, instead turning and walking toward the front entrance of the church. He could hear her footsteps behind him and smiled. There might be hope for her yet.

He had imagined this moment over and over again during the last couple of days. This was to be the Bishop's triumphant return to the church, and he'd never imagined that it would be his responsibility to see it through. He felt the weight on his shoulders and knew that he couldn't allow himself to fail.

He pushed the main door open and went inside.

There were eight people in the central area of the church. He could see them spread out when he first stepped through the door. Several sat in pews and two milled around, speaking quietly.

He would have come during a more packed service, except he wasn't sure how Megyn would react to what he was about to do. This was as much for her sake as for the mission.

"Stay close," he ordered, striding up through the pews to the front dais.

He climbed confidently up the steps to the podium and then turned back to face the gathered audience. Most of them were engrossed in their own thoughts or prayers and didn't even notice him standing there. He saw one woman elbow her husband then nod discretely up at him, a smile on her face.

He would take joy in wiping that smile away.

"Greetings," he called out. His hands were shaking

and sweaty with nerves and his voice was higher pitched than he would have liked. He cleared his throat. "May I have your attention please?"

A few of them glanced up at him, some curious and others annoyed, but in general the response was tepid and underwhelming.

"My name is Jeremy Caldwell, and this is my friend Megyn Wilford. We're here today because our dear father and mentor once presided over this church. His name was Leopold Glasser. You might have heard of him. His duty was to lead you to the hand of God so that you might all find eternal salvation."

He heard movement from off to his left and then a side door opened up.

"Young man, this is a house of God and you are disturbing these people. You need to sit down—"

Without looking, he held up his right hand and silenced the priest. He didn't need the hand movement, as his actual control was mental, but he knew it made him look a lot more intimidating. He reached into the priest's mind and seized control.

Wills pitted against each other, the priest didn't stand a chance: so much for him being a bastion of strength for the Lord.

The priest froze mid-sentence, choking on the words, and the action had the desired effect. The crowed perked up immediately. Eyes went wide and people shifted in their seats, not with fear but rather confusion.

Confusion was good enough for now. Fear wouldn't be far behind.

He lowered his hand.

"Where was I before I was so rudely interrupted? Ah, yes. Our Father. Our dear Father once served as the shepherd to this flock, until you so heinously turned against him. He was a good man, and you heathens caused him much pain and suffering with your lies. We are here to rectify that."

He turned to Megyn and beckoned for her to step up next to him. Her eyes widened: she disliked being the focus of his attention.

That didn't matter, though. When push came to shove, he was confident she would make the right decision. He walked down a few steps, gently took her hand, and guided her back up to the top. Then, he turned her around to face the crowd.

"These people," he explained softly to her, "accused our Father of terrible crimes. They made up stories and lies, and those lies hurt him and damaged his credibility within the church."

"They did?"

"Yes. They called him a molester and a philanderer. They said he preached against the bible and they turned him into an outcast. These heathens caused him no end of torment and pain. They need to be punished."

He could feel Megyn staring at him but refused to make eye contact. Instead, he continued scanning at the crowd. Another man stood up from the third row of pews back, dirty and disheveled.

"Kid, I don't know what the hell you're going on about—"

Jeremy reached out and seized him mentally as well, this time not just to silence him, but rather to sit him back down. The man let out a groan and then collapsed back into the pew.

A few other churchgoers shifted in their seats and gasped, but no one else stood.

"Have you been practicing?" he asked Megyn.

"What Father taught you to do ... have you been practicing?"

"Yes, on Sheila, but I've never actually—"

"This is the moment you've been preparing for. Everything you have done, it has all led to this."

"Jeremy, I don't think—"

"Do you want to let our Father down?"

"No, of course not."

"Then do it," he said.

"I can't."

He glanced over the crowd and picked out a small woman sitting about eight rows back. Her mousy nose and cheeks made it clear she wouldn't put up much of a fight. He pointed out the woman and then turned back to Megyn.

"Her."

He reached out and seized the old woman's mind, planting the suggestion to walk up to the front of the church. She resisted, and he could feel her mentally screaming out for help, but he easily subdued her.

The woman stood up slowly from the pew and walked up the center aisle. Her blank face belied the internal struggle. She came to stop in front of them, about five feet away at the bottom of the stairs.

"Her first," he reiterated. "Just do what Father taught you."

"I don't—"

He shot a glare at Megyn, getting frustrated. He almost reached out to her mind to force her to do it.

Almost.

First, Leopold had made him swear to never use his abilities against the other children. They were his family, his brothers and sisters, and they were never to betray one another no matter what happened. That family included Megyn and he took the promise seriously.

Secondly, though, he had already tried before.

A few years earlier, before Megyn had been stationed out here in Ohio and when they were all still living with the Bishop, he had tried to use his power to control Megyn. He had attempted to dominate her with his mental abilities, figuring she would be a push over and he could make her do embarrassing things.

She wasn't a pushover. His abilities had almost no effect on her except to piss her off. She had broken both of his arms and his nose with her telekinetic abilities before Leopold had finally subdued her. Jeremy was in the hospital for weeks.

She had forgotten about that incident, but he never had.

"We need to do this. These people were cruel to our Father. Do you want to let them get away with it?"

Never mind that no one in this room had ever known the Bishop, though. Jeremy decided to keep that part to himself. Leopold's service here was brief and before many of these parishioner's time.

A handful might know him, if only by reputation, but that didn't matter. It was their families and friends who had hurt him, which made them guilty by association.

"Do what our father taught you to do, or I'll do something worse."

Megyn cowered against his glare, and he knew from the look in her eyes that he'd won. She turned back to face the old woman, lifting up her hand, and then she made a clenching motion.

It happened slowly, and at first he couldn't tell if Megyn was doing anything or not. Then, he heard the old woman start choking. She clutched at her throat, pulling at invisible fingers that weren't there. Her eyes popped open in terror as she realized what was happening and she struggled, stumbling backwards against one of the pews.

Jeremy battered away her feeble attempts to free herself from his mental grip and watched in satisfaction as the life fled from her eyes.

The rest of the room erupted in panic as people rushed for the exits. They began screaming and shouting at one another and trying to get away.

Megyn waved her other hand in the air, and all of the doors slammed shut. Another motion and she knocked the running people to the ground. Jeremy watched in satisfaction, impressed as always by the sheer raw power Megyn possessed.

She kept her focus squarely on the old woman in the center of the aisle, eyes narrowed.

Suddenly, the old woman sucked in a rasping and ragged breath or air, collapsing to her knees and clutching her throat. She sucked in another breath and coughed.

"What's going on?" Jeremy asked. "What's happening?"

"I can't do it," Megyn replied, a tear streaming down her cheeks. "That is where I always stopped with Sheila and I ... I can't go any farther."

"What? What do you mean you can't do it?"

She turned to face him, a pleading look in her eyes. "I can't do this, Jeremy. Please, don't make me. I don't want to hurt her."

He felt anger building in the pit of his stomach. "Are you joking? After what they did to our Father, you can't punish them? You are weak, Megyn. You never loved him. You never loved the man who took you in and protected you, did you?"

"Don't say that!"

"It's true, though, isn't it? Your heart was never really in this. After everything he did for you, this is how you repay him? Weak and ungrateful child."

"Jeremy—"

"I told him we shouldn't trust you but he didn't believe me. He saw something in you, and here you are letting him down. But, no matter. I can take care of things if you won't, because I actually loved our father."

"Don't—"

"But, I told you that if you couldn't do it, it would be worse for them," he said. "This was your responsibility, but if you can't handle it, then I have to, and now it will be much worse. Just remember: this was your fault."

He turned back to the priest, still stuck in his mental grip. The weak willed man was simple to control, and Jeremy had to admit that the power he held over the priest felt good. He could feel the man flailing and crying out in his mind, though outwardly he seemed perfectly calm and relaxed.

He would have been the perfect vessel for a demon, one that Jeremy could easily fill with one of his soldiers. The demons weren't ready, though, and he was still missing crucial components for the summoning rituals. Right now, however, he just needed an example for Megyn.

He saw an oil lamp and a lighter lying on a table in the corner of the church. It seemed to be about half full with liquid

He grinned.

"There," he said, pointing at the table. The verbal

command wasn't necessary, but he knew he had an audience.

The priest strode over to the corner of the room and stood next to the table.

"Pick up the oil."

"Jeremy, what are you doing?" Megyn whispered.

He ignored her. The priest did as he said, lifting the lamp off the table.

"Unscrew the lid and pour it over yourself."

"Stop this," Megyn pleaded, grabbing his arm. He shook her loose and had eyes only for the priest. The man fought back harder now, a sudden burst of willpower as he realized what was happening …

As well as what was about to happen.

Jeremy struggled mentally to subdue him. It was harder this time around, and he felt a headache building in the back of his mind from extended use of his abilities. He fought the pain away: it would be over soon.

"Pick up the lighter and ignite it. Careful, don't get it too close to your clothes … yet."

The priest's hand shook as he followed Jeremy's command. Jeremy could feel his will breaking as the poor fool realized the futility of what he was doing. Jeremy was too strong, too practiced, and it was almost done.

The priest flicked the lighter, holding the flame away from his oil soaked clothing. Jeremy took a moment to savor it: the priest wasn't very old, in his late twenties probably, with dark hair and skinny features. Terror and understanding filled his eyes, but he was helpless to stop it.

"Jeremy … please … please don't do this," Megyn whispered.

"You wanted this," Jeremy replied. "You had one responsibility, and you couldn't even do that."

"I'll do it. I'll do it. I'll do anything you want. Please, just don't do this."

He turned to face Megyn. She cried, eyes full of fear. He reached out and gently took her hand between his, patting it.

He smiled at her.

"Too late."

A final mental command and suddenly the room erupted in heat as the priest touched the lighter against his chest. Shocked screams and gasps sounded from out on the main floor of the church and more people scrambled for the exits. The locked doors held, however, so there was nowhere to go.

The flame spread slowly, climbing across the man's clothing. Jeremy felt a flash of pain inside the priest's mind and it broke Jeremy's grip on him. The priest started screaming and fell to the floor, rolling across the carpet, but the oil kept burning and the fire kept spreading.

The smell, Jeremy realized, was the craziest experience of his life. It filled the church as though they were standing next to a pig roast, and the most disgusting part was that it didn't actually smell terrible. He hadn't eaten in a while, and he could feel his stomach rumbling.

He hadn't expected that, and he quickly pushed the feeling away. He certainly wasn't a cannibal, and this was vengeance and not something for him to enjoy. He was getting revenge on these people for what they did to his father, and they were only the first step in getting redemption for everything that had happened to his father.

Megyn was shaking as she watched the priest burn on the floor. The rest of the people in the Church watched in horror as well, barely moving.

It only lasted a few moments before the fire burned itself out and the priest went still, smoldering on the carpet. Much of the skin of his face and chest had melted.

Megyn suddenly realized Jeremy still held her hand and jerked it free.

"How could you ...?"

"The rest?" he asked. "Would you like to do your job now, or should I take care of them for you, too?"

She flashed him a look full of rage and terror and he thought for a moment that she might actually attack him. He nearly winced at the prospect of her blow, but managed to keep his expression calm. This was the moment of truth, because he knew if she did attack him he wouldn't be able to stop her.

The things she could do to him...

She didn't strike him, though. Underneath the rage was a profound sense of confusion and fear at what he had just done. It left a weakness in her that he'd come to expect from Megyn, and he smiled in satisfaction. She wasn't a leader, nor was she a brave soldier.

She would obey, though.

"OK. I'll do it."

She turned to face the remaining people. Her motion seemed to jolt them back to life and they started fleeing again. Two of them banged and jerked on the front door of the church, struggling to pry it open against her mental grip. They might as well have been trying to break through a brick wall.

She held up her hand, and one of the men

pounding on the door started to clutch his throat, making choking noises.

"You're doing this for Father."

She didn't answer him, just continued choking the life out of the man. Tears streamed down her cheeks and she sniffled.

The man collapsed to the ground, eyes glossy, and the man next to him started grabbing at his throat as well. Jeremy watched, pleased, as that man died.

"How many?" she asked.

"All of them."

She sobbed, turning to face the old woman she'd first begun choking. The woman cowered in the third row of pews, crying.

She began making choking noises, and a minute later it was over, too.

"Good work, sister," Jeremy said, patting Megyn on the shoulder as she silently moved on to the next worshipper. Megyn jerked away under his touch, but that was alright. She didn't have to like him, she just needed to do her job. "Very good."

***

Megyn refused to make eye contact with Jeremy after they finally vacated the church. She sat slumped in the seat and stared out the window. They waited in the car for nearly an hour while their demonic driver went inside and harvested the people Megyn had killed. This was the part Jeremy disliked the most, and the main reason he kept the demon around. Cutting on bodies was inelegant and laborious.

Megyn might not be taking things well, but Jeremy was euphoric. It was the happiest moment of his life.

He'd gotten vengeance for his mentor and father figure and also exerted his dominance over Megyn.

She never would have agreed to any of this if she'd known his plan, but there was just enough pressure and provocation in the moment to turn her into an accomplice.

She couldn't take it back now. She had killed those people. In for a penny, in for a pound, and there was no going back. She wouldn't cause him any more trouble, and he was quite pleased to have such a powerful ally.

She might be in a funk right now, but in time she would come to see that what they had done was not only necessary, but also beautiful. They had managed to not only punish these parishioners for what they had done to Leopold, but also make use of their deaths in a meaningful way that would help them achieve their final goal. Those deaths would have meaning well beyond anything that had come before.

The driver was covered in blood when he returned to the car. He put the organs in the trunk and climbed into the front seat. The organs were in an ice chest which would be full of the important bits that Jeremy would need to summon his demons.

He'd never done the ritual alone so he prepared the harvest. He'd helped the Bishop do it many times in the past so he was confident he could make it work after a little trial and error.

As they drove away, Jeremy could still smell the burning priest and his charred flesh. Though he didn't know if he imagined the smell or not. He figured it was probably bits and flakes of the man that had gotten caught in his nasal cavity.

"I know you don't like doing this and that you are afraid," Jeremy said once they left the Church, "but today you did a great thing. Our Father would have been proud."

Megyn fell silent for a long while, staring out the window. Tears continued to stream down her cheeks but she no longer sobbed.

They drove back toward their hideout while Jeremy tried to decide on their next move. He had the supplies, so now he just needed the vessels to bring in his demon army. Once they began attacking and people began dying the world would have no choice but to watch and—

"What did you mean when you said he 'would have been proud'?" Megyn asked suddenly, shifting sharply in the seat to face him. "You said he would have been, not that he is or will be?"

Jeremy waved his hand in the air, dismissing her concern. "I just meant if he was here right now."

"No, you didn't. Back at the church when you were giving your little speech, you said he was a good man. Not that he is a good man, but that he was. What happened? Where is our Father?"

"He's overseas planning—"

"Don't lie to me," Megyn interrupted, grabbing his arm. "Stop lying to me, Jeremy. What happened?"

He took a steadying breath, cursing himself at the slip. He thought to lie to her again, but he knew that in this tender moment he needed to be careful.

"He is dead. They murdered him."

Her eyes went wide. "Who?"

"A priest and his lackey. They found us when we were leaving the country and they killed our Father. That's why I came here, so we could continue his legacy and finish what he started."

Megyn took a moment to mentally process what he

was saying. "No, no, that can't…"

She trailed off, her face contorting. Jeremy leaned over and wrapped his arm around her, pulling her close to his chest. She struggled a tiny bit, but then she embraced him back and cried onto his shoulder.

"There, there, little sister. It's OK. It will all be OK."

She cried on his shoulder, squeezing him tightly, and he could feel her tears running down his arm.

"Why didn't you tell me?" she asked finally. "When you first got here. Why lie about it?"

"I didn't want to hurt you," he said. "I wanted to protect you, little sister. We are family. I was worried how you might take it."

Anger flashed across her face. "How I might take it? What is that supposed to mean?"

"We don't have time to grieve," he explained softly, using his finger to push a strand of hair out of her face. He leaned in and kissed her cheek, tasting her salty tears. "Dear sister, we can't afford any distractions until this is over with. We will grieve for our father, but right now we need discipline."

"They murdered our father. What we need is vengeance."

"And we will have it. I promise you we will have it against all of them."

Megyn fell quiet, head lying against Jeremy's chest. He gently stroked her hair. He hated discussing the death of the Bishop, but it was nice having the truth off of his chest. Maybe his slip was for the best: he wouldn't need to lie to her anymore, and now he could confide in Megyn.

"You didn't have to kill the priest like that."

"I know," he said. "I'm just angry about losing our father and I wanted to lash out."

"He didn't deserve—"

"He deserved that and so much more. What they did to Leopold was terrible, Megyn. It was a secret he didn't want you to know, but these people were very cruel to him. We cannot allow them to—"

"We have a problem."

The interruption came from the front of the car as the driver pulled it to a stop. They were near to the home base where Megyn had been living these past months, which meant the second half of his plan was beginning.

He really had to sell it.

"What's wrong?"

"Someone has been here," the demon lied.

Of course they couldn't see anything from outside the old service station to give him that idea, but that wasn't the point. "Who?"

The demon looked at Jeremy in the rearview mirror. He saw the man's eyes.

"The priest and the hunter. The ones who killed Leopold. They were here."

Megyn gasped, pulling free of Jeremy to look ahead. The driver slowly pulled the car forward. "We should check it out," Jeremy said. "Do you think they are gone?"

"Hard to say, but yes," the demon offered. "I don't think they are here anymore."

"Sheila," Megyn breathed, jumping out of the still moving car and sprinting for the front door to the service station.

Jeremy waited until she was gone and then looked back at the mirror. "You got all the organs, right?"

"Yes sir. I hacked them up so it wouldn't be too obvious."

"Good. Stay here."

He climbed out of the car to follow Megyn inside, and then hesitated. "And, clean yourself up. We're staying in a hotel tonight instead of this dump and I don't need you blood stained and disheveled when you rent us the room."

Then, he closed the door and walked slowly into the service station. He found Megyn just inside the backroom, collapsed in a ball and staring at the three bodies of her friends.

The demon wasn't lying: he'd done a number on these bodies. Brutal work, hacking them apart, and it turned his stomach a little bit. He wondered how things would look back at the Church.

"I'm so sorry," he whispered, kneeling next to her.

She turned and threw herself into his arms. "Jeremy, they're dead!"

He held her and rubbed her back. "I'm sorry. The priest must have followed us here. It's terrible."

She kept crying, and he held her for several more minutes. He hoped she didn't notice the missing organs or look any closer at the victims.

Finally, she pulled loose and looked him in the eyes.

"How could they...?"

"They are evil, sis. They won't stop until we are all dead."

"I want them to pay for this. Promise me that we will kill them."

He struggled to keep himself from smiling. "I promise."

Chapter 5

"We need to hurry, Abigail," Frieda called out, stuffing a wrinkled blue blouse into her bags. She hated having things just lying around, preferring to keep the hotel room tidy.

The clock on the table told her they were going to be late for their meeting with Mikael. They needed to get back onto the road and across the city in the next couple of minutes.

"I'm not going to tell you again!"

She glanced behind her and saw that the bathroom door was still closed. Inside she heard the shower running and the eight-year-old girl singing at the top of her lungs. She sighed. "Am I just talking to myself out here?"

No reply.

The answer was 'yes.'

It was something she was getting more and more used to doing, as it were. Abigail listened to her, sure, but only when she felt like it. She was as hard-headed and stubborn of a person as Frieda had ever met. She even rivaled Arthur sometimes in how stubborn she could be.

Sometimes.

Frieda warned her twenty minutes ago that they needed to get back on the road as soon as possible. Abigail even agreed, and yet here she was taking a thirty-minute hot shower. Frieda didn't even know why she bothered trying to convince the little girl how important their mission was: Abigail got ready when she damn well felt like it.

That wasn't to say Frieda didn't enjoy the constant arguing and bickering with her little companion. She had enjoyed these past months on the road with her. Compared to her solitary life, it was quite nice having a companion. Of course, if Frieda had been asked six months ago if she would eventually enjoy having Abigail around, the answer would have been a resounding 'no.'

Frieda walked over to the bathroom door and banged her fist against it.

"Hurry up in there! We need to be on the road ten minutes ago!"

"Alright, alright!"

To be honest, Abigail taking her time didn't really bother Frieda that much. She was just happy the girl was strong willed enough to be feisty and enjoy life. After what happened to her back in West Virginia before Arthur rescued her ...

Part of Frieda was afraid the little girl would never recover.

Abigail's lackadaisical attitude wouldn't have bothered her at all, in fact, if it wasn't for the reason that Frieda was actually about to go out in the field on a mission. Frieda was used to pushing papers and organizing assets these last five or so years, so the idea of being back out on a hunt was thrilling.

Even if her target wasn't much of a threat.

Her phone started to buzz in her pocket. She slipped it loose, read the name, and sighed. It was Garfield, one of her hunters. He was out in South Dakota chasing one of the Bishop's other children.

Garfield was also still pissed at Arthur for everything that went down at the water treatment plant, and he was also more than a little unhappy with her as well. She sympathized: she wasn't thrilled about how things went down, either.

She flipped the phone open and accepted the call. "Hello, Garfield."

"I got the kid. What do you want me to do with her?"

"Nice to hear from you, too. How are things?" she asked sarcastically.

He didn't answer. Looks like he wasn't quite ready to forgive her just yet. Frieda sighed.

"Head down to South Florida."

"Florida? That's like seven hours away."

"We have another child out there for you to track down. This one's a teenager and has been starting fires. Already killed five people."

"Alright. What do I do with this one?"

"You mean Maggie? She has a name."

"Sure? Where am I dumping her? The sooner the better: she keeps trying to bite me."

Frieda almost laughed, but caught herself at the last moment. Garfield was a sensitive man and definitely didn't consider what he just said to be funny.

"I'm not sure yet. I'll have to phone it in to the Vatican and see what they want to do with her."

"Great," he replied flatly. "And how long will that take?"

She ignored him. "I'll call you back with a drop off point along your way as soon as I get ahold of the Church."

"Fine. And what am I supposed to do to keep her from biting me until then?"

"Slather yourself in pepper sauce? That'll keep you safe unless she likes spicy food."

He hung up. Frieda burst out laughing. It would be a while before Garfield forgave her for pulling him off his last mission and everything Arthur did to him, but eventually he'd get over it. It was all a balancing act, and one she perfected over the years with the Hunters.

The shower turned off, though it was still a couple of minutes before Abigail finally emerged from the bathroom. Steam billowed out of the room around her like she was an angel making a grand entrance. Frieda only sighed and shook her head.

"Are you ready to go?"

"Almost," Abigail replied, rushing over and grabbing a pair of dirty socks off of a chair. She quickly slid them on her feet, bouncing on one foot at a time and nearly falling over.

Frieda pointed at her watch. "We need to be on the road. I have an appointment to keep."

"I know, I know."

"Do you? If we get there too late then we aren't going to be able to—"

Her phone started to ring again. She looked at it in frustration and saw that it was another hunter. This one, Charles Greathouse, was in Michigan dealing with yet another threat.

"Hello?"

"Hey, Frieda. Quick question: how the hell am I supposed to stop a kid who can see the future? Every time we figure out where she's going, we get there about an hour too late."

"What are you talking about?"

"The kid you assigned me is clairvoyant. She knows my every move before I make it. Me and my wife are both out of ideas for how to stop her."

"Just think one step ahead."

"That is the worst advice anyone has ever given me. One step ahead today is still in the past for tomorrow, which she knows."

"What advice would you prefer? I've never dealt with a clairvoyant anything, much less one who is a child. I don't know: do something unpredictable."

He laughed, but there was no mirth in it. He was clearly annoyed and wanted to take out his frustration on her.

She was used to that: being a punching bag was about half of her job, and she was careful not to let it get to her. It was totally understandable: the work of her hunters was perilous, and the worse it was the more frustrated they got.

Danger led to emotion and emotion to frustration, and that often meant she was a target for them when they were feeling down or annoyed.

She had to admit, though, that Charles had more reason than most to be annoyed with her: this kid he was after was definitely going to be difficult to track down, which is why she assigned it to him. He and his wife were some of her best Hunters, besides Arthur.

"The future is still predictable, even when it's unpredictable," he said. "I can't be unpredictable when no matter what I do has already happened and is therefore predicted."

"I don't know. Just keep at it. Eventually you'll wear her down and she'll just give up."

"How long will that take?"

"No idea. A year? Maybe two?"

"Not funny."

"It's a little funny."

"I'm sick of this kid and just chasing her all across the state."

"Has she done anything dangerous?"

"No. That's the thing. She isn't doing anything at all except running from me. It's like she thinks this is a game and she's having fun messing with me and—"

"Well then stick with it," Frieda said. "If it's a game and she isn't hurting people, then you must be winning."

"You know that doesn't help me at all Frieda and I—"

"Gotta go!"

She hung up and slipped the phone into her pocket.

Abigail was standing in the center of the room, still bent over and balancing on one leg, her second sock dangling from her hand and mouth hanging open in shock. Suddenly, she grinned at Frieda and then burst out laughing.

"What's so funny?"

"You are."

Frieda didn't think she was that funny. She frowned at Abigail. "Are you ready?"

"Hang on. I still have to pack my bag."

"I already packed it."

"You didn't pack it right."

Frieda groaned. "This is cutting into our breakfast time."

"That's fine. I don't like breakfast anyway."

"Well, I do."

Abigail just shrugged and kept re-packing her belongings. Frieda doubted it would take long to gather up their target and get back on the road. With any luck, it would be wrapped up by this afternoon.

She tapped the phone against her leg thoughtfully. The target Charles was chasing wasn't one of the higher threat targets that the Vatican was worried about. She wasn't much of a danger on her own, and even the Bishop wrote that little girl off as a hopeless cause in his journals.

She still needed to be caught, though. All of them did, which was why Frieda was out here in Minnesota with Abigail. They were chasing after another little boy, fifteen years old, who also wasn't considered to be much of a threat. His name was Curtis, and from all reports this should be an easy job.

All of Frieda's other assets were out working on much more dangerous cases, which was why she didn't have the luxury of sitting this one out.

The church doubted her, though, to work this alone: the Vatican sent over a priest of their own to help capture Curtis and bring him back home. His powers, from everything Bishop Glasser documented in his journal, were empathic in nature. He read emotions, but little else.

The Church didn't consider him a threat, but he was considered a high value target, which was why they sent one of their own to help acquire him.

"Alright, I'm ready," Abigail said, hefting her bag off the bed. "We can go now."

"We can?" Frieda asked sarcastically. "That's fantastic..."

***

The man who was waiting for them in the little diner wasn't quite what Frieda expected. Mikael was short, balding, and with more than a little bit of pudge around his waistline. He was in his mid-forties at least, and the expression on his face was one of serious deliberation. The face of a man who rarely laughed or smiled.

He didn't look much like a priest, in fact, but more like a monk. The Vatican hadn't given her much information about him, just explaining that he was in the area and she was to follow his orders.

"You are Frieda Gotlieb?" he asked as they approached

"Yes. You are Mikael? They didn't give me a last name."

"You don't need one. I've been waiting."

"I know," Frieda said, shooting a glance at Abigail. "We apologize."

The man dismissed her apology with a curt wave of his hand and gestured for them to sit down. The smell of pancakes and coffee in the air was making Frieda's mouth water and she was starving.

"Did you already order?"

"I don't eat while the sun is out," the man said. His tone made it clear that he thought Frieda's question was ignorant.

"Do you mind if we order something, then?"

Annoyance flashed across his face and then waved his hand again. "Of course not. Do as you will."

The waiter came by and took their order. She and Abigail both got small breakfast plates, hers with coffee and Abigail's with orange juice. She wanted desperately to order the chocolate waffle breakfast but changed her mind when she saw them on another table. They were small and soggy, so she stuck with the eggs and bacon.

"To business, then?" she asked after the waiter stepped away from the table.

Mikael looked pointedly over at Abigail. "Perhaps we shouldn't speak openly."

"You can speak freely in front of Abi. She's with me and I trust her completely."

"She is a child."

"You were one as well, once."

She almost added 'I assume,' but changed her

mind. He seemed to take offense at the suggestion, and then merely shrugged noncommittally.

"Very well. I've been tracking our target for the last few hours but haven't managed to isolate him. He's managed to evade all attempts at tracking."

"Curtis is an empath," Frieda replied. "How much damage can he do?"

"He is known to be an empath," the priest disagreed, "but that doesn't mean it is his only ability. We should approach cautiously and assume there is more to him than we anticipate."

Frieda disagreed, but she didn't voice her concern aloud.

Her phone started to ring. It was another of her agents, this one working in Texas.

"Sorry, I have to take this."

The priest turned away and stare out the window of the diner. Frieda stepped over to an empty area of the restaurant and then accepted the call. Another hunter asking for a drop off point for his target.

The call didn't take long, only a couple of minutes for a status report and some information, and then she walked back over to the table. Her food was there, and Abigail was already almost done eating.

The priest watched the young girl devour her food with a look of morbid fascination on his face, as though amazed someone so little ate so much. Abigail didn't even seem to notice.

"So, what is our plan of action?"

"We will wait and watch to determine what the child's intention is. When we deem the opportunity safe, we will capture him and I will relocate him to the Vatican."

"Alright," Frieda said. "What do you want us to

do?"

"I want you to stay out of the way and await my call. Stay nearby and ready. Nothing more."

Frieda was a little frustrated that he didn't want her help after all, but not surprised. Very few people in his position liked the Council of Chaldea, much less her Hunters. They were a nuisance at best, and looked down upon by many within the Church.

Their affiliation was a loose one and the Church only turned to them in times of peril or to solve dangerous situations. Frieda knew that after everything that happened over the last few weeks their situation deteriorated and the existence of the Council was in serious jeopardy. What she didn't need to do right now was make new enemies from within the church itself.

So, she wouldn't argue.

"Sounds good," she agreed. "We will get a hotel room nearby and you have my number. Let me know if you need anything."

"I will," he said.

Then, without further word, he stood up and disappeared out of the diner. Frieda watched him go and then let out a groan.

"He's kind of a jerk," Abigail said, sipping her orange juice.

"I know," Frieda replied, taking a bite out of a strip of bacon. Suddenly, she wasn't very hungry. "I guess that means we're going to have some downtime to just hang out and relax—"

Her phone buzzed on the table. She glanced at it and saw that yet another hunter was calling. She'd been dealing with more problems over the last week than the entire last year combined.

She sighed. "It never ends, does it?"

Abigail stared at her, a solemn expression on her young face. Frieda was glad that at least Abigail understood how frustrating her situation was.

Or, at least she thought the girl did.

Instead, Abigail pointed down at Frieda's plate and her last strip of bacon.

"Are you going to eat that?"

Chapter 6

Arthur was glad that Niccolo was finally starting to crawl out of his lethargic state. The priest wasn't as withdrawn or sullen as he was over the last few days of driving and seemed to be taking the mission seriously.

He knew from personal experience that the only way to deal with the sort of trauma Niccolo was facing was to stay busy. After his family was murdered he threw himself back into his work. It was a mistake that had led to his first negative interaction with Niccolo many months earlier. Niccolo had seen him at his lowest, only days after he murdered those cultists in West Virginia. He regretted what had happened, but it kept him from doing anything even worse.

Like committing suicide.

Arthur didn't like to admit it, but he seriously considered taking his own life in those first weeks after his family had died. Charging into the manor in West Virginia was something of a suicide mission, one he never intended to survive, but he planned out even more visceral ways of doing it with either guns, knives, or pills.

He might have done it, too, had he never stumbled across Abigail. She was like a beacon of light in the darkness, though if he was being completely honest it had nothing at all to do with her. She was the epitome of an idea: the idea that other people in the world still needed his help.

That realization saved his life and gave him a renewed sense of purpose, and he just hoped that Niccolo could find a similar beacon to pull him out of his darkness. He was busy for now, but once the mission was over he would have time to fix things. Plenty of time to think and reminisce, and if he wasn't careful he might find himself on a dark path.

Part of what was happening, Arthur knew, was Jeremy acting off the cuff and making rash decisions. Whatever plan the Bishop concocted, it died with him, and now the child was just trying to make the best of a bad situation. The teenage boy was apt to make a mistake that Arthur might capitalize on.

It just hadn't happened yet.

Arthur still had no clue how he would stop Jeremy once they finally caught up to him, if they ever did. Whatever mental ability Jeremy used to invade his mind back at the shipyard, Arthur had no real defense against it. He'd managed to fight off the control, but barely, and even then Jeremy caused him to lose track of time. Even if it was only seconds, in a gunfight those precious seconds could mean the difference between life and death.

They were just pulling into the parking lot of the church in Akron, Ohio when his phone started to ring. It was Frieda finally calling him back.

"Hello?"

"Hello, Arthur. How are things going?"

"I'm fine, but how are you? Are you dodging my calls?"

"No."

"You sent me to voicemail twice."

"Because, I don't have any answers for you. I knew what you wanted to ask and decided to spare us both the time. Plus, I've been busy on my end. I'm on a job myself."

"No kidding?"

"Don't sound so surprised," she replied with a laugh. "I'm not only an administrator."

"Oh, I know. I've been telling you for years to get back out there on a hunt. Your skills are practically gone. I just never really thought you would do it."

"Well, circumstances haven't given me much of a choice. More people are dying every hour and the Church demands results. After everything Leopold did to us monetarily, we can't afford to sit this one out."

"So, you're hunting."

"Even I can't stay on the bench this time. Any luck on locating Jeremy? What did you find out at the Church?"

"Nothing yet," he admitted. "We only just got to Akron."

"The Vatican priest I spoke to sounded a little frantic when he called me earlier. Whatever it is, it's probably pretty bad. Hurry up and deal with that threat. I could really use your help on another job right about now."

"It's that bad?'

"You have no idea. The kid I'm after is an empath, but we're having trouble keeping up with the demand. We've had a dozen incidents reported around the country. Six of them aren't even being tracked yet. I've pulled every asset and the Church has called in all of the support they can get, but it feels like we're several steps behind."

"Is anyone on damage control?"

"The rest of the Council is helping the Vatican deal with the fallout. We're spinning everything and trying to stay ahead of it. So far no one has connected any dots or found hard evidence to prove what's happening, but there are a lot of stories floating around."

With this many attacks across the country it would be hard for the public to stay unaware, Arthur knew, but something like a psychic child was impossible to prove. People might tell family and friends about the things that they saw, but as long as the authorities denied anything happened and there was no solid proof, it would all eventually go away.

"Jeremy is the one we need to worry about," Arthur said. "Plus whoever he came here to Ohio to meet. These were the two children that Leopold was expecting the most out of, and if we keep them out of the spotlight then the rest shouldn't be too hard to round up."

"I know. I'm just worried about what Jeremy might do. If he's half as strong as you say he is, he's going to be hard to cover up."

"Is the church sending backup?"

"Not yet. There isn't anyone to send, and since nothing has happened in Ohio, at least until this church thing, they don't want to waste resources."

"So, we're on our own?"

"For now."

"Great. I think the first wave of attacks was a distraction," Arthur said. "We're doing exactly what Jeremy hoped we would do. He wants to spread our resources thin so we aren't prepared to deal with whatever is happening here."

"That's where you come in, Arthur. We might be spread out and desperate, but if you're our last line of defense you can't fail."

"I don't plan to," Arthur replied.

He parked the car and shifted in the seat to face Niccolo. He put his hand over the phone receiver, and then said to the priest, "Go and take a look around. I'll be right behind you."

Niccolo nodded. He climbed out of the car and began walking across the church's gravel parking lot toward the white church. Arthur waited until he was out of earshot before speaking to Frieda again.

"We're at Saint Thomas Church checking things out. I'm not sure if this was Jeremy or the other kid, but there are a lot of police cars and ambulances out here. Five body bags at least."

"Call me when you figure it all out."

"I will."

Arthur hung up the phone and climbed out of the car to go and find Niccolo. The front entrance to the church was open and he found Niccolo just inside the doorway. The priest was locked in place and surveying the devastation in front of him with a horrified look on his face.

The first thing Arthur noticed as he walked up beside him was the smell. It was burnt flesh, and human at that. Arthur had only smelled it a few times in his life, but it never got any less disgusting.

It only took a few seconds to spot the source of the odor: a smoldering mess in the corner of the room that used to be a man. The fire charred the outside of his skin and clothes, but the pain must have been unbearable before he died.

"The priest," Arthur said, barely making out the man's attire. "Looks like he was burned alive."

"Who could do something like this?" Niccolo whispered. His voice wavered and was barely audible. Arthur reached out and placed a steadying hand on his shoulder.

"A monster."

"A child," Niccolo objected, turning to face him. "A

child did this, but also a monster. I used to think the two were mutually exclusive."

"I wish they were."

From the outside, this little church had reminded Arthur of Saint Joseph's Cathedral back in Everett, Washington, the one that Father Reynolds presided over. This one was about the same size and built in a similar architectural style.

The exterior façade, however, was where the resemblance ended.

Inside, the church was a disaster. Many people died here, and they died horribly. The bodies were gone except for that of the burnt priest and a few others. Much of their spilled blood had seeped into the hardwood flooring and made the entire church floor slippery.

The remaining bodies and body bags, though, were what caught Arthur's eye. His original estimation of five people murdered here was low he realized.

There must have been ten of them in here originally, at least, though with the amount of damage that was done to the ones that were left it was difficult to tell. Someone had cut these people open, removed their organs and intestines and scattered them around the room to cover the Christian murals and paintings on the walls.

Blood and gore covered the entire interior of the church, mostly dry now. Some of the organs, Arthur noted on a closer inspection, were missing.

Just like the people back in Everett.

"Who could do something like this? Child or not, this is terrible."

Arthur didn't have a good answer. He'd seen a lot of horrible things in his time as a Hunter for the

Council of Chaldea, but this level of brutality took it all to a whole other place. A practiced hand had dismembered these parishioners, and it took a fair amount of time.

He doubted Jeremy did it: at his age, he wouldn't have the upper body strength, and no matter how jaded the teenager was about life Arthur highly doubted he had the stomach for this level of brutality.

The little girl he was traveling with? Not a chance.

Which meant the culprit was no doubt whatever humans or demons were traveling with Jeremy. He assumed someone got Jeremy out of California, but this all but guaranteed he wasn't working alone.

That made things dangerous enough, but with the organs he collected here, Jeremy could bring many more demonic soldiers into the world.

No one was safe.

"They are misguided," he offered. He knew it was small consolation to the priest.

"That doesn't change what they've done. Nor does it excuse something like this."

"I know," Arthur agreed. "There is no excuse."

Normally, he would have added some empty platitude for Niccolo about how it wasn't the children's fault, and that they could be saved, but right now he simply couldn't find the words.

One of the officers on scene took notice of them and began walking their way. He was distracted and unfocused, clearly upset by the carnage he was witnessing. Arthur slipped a fake badge out of his pocket he'd used in countless similar situations.

"Can I help you gentlemen with something?"

Arthur held up the badge. "Yeah. I'm Detective Simmons with the FBI. This is Father Niccolo Paladina.

He's here on behalf of the Catholic Church as a consultant to this crime."

The cop glanced at the badge but didn't pay much attention to it. Arthur quickly slipped it away.

Niccolo flashed Arthur a confused look but Arthur ignored the gaze of the priest. The cop didn't seem to notice.

"A consultant? Does the church think this was some sort of occult crime?"

It took a second for Niccolo to realize the man was addressing him. He cleared his throat.

"We aren't sure yet."

"This is a preliminary investigation," Arthur added. "We're looking into the incident that took place here to find out more information before making any determinations. What can you tell us?"

"Not a lot," the officer admitted, turning back toward the devastation. "Whoever chopped these people up was strong. Like, really strong. The knife he used wasn't that sharp."

"Hacking up bodies like this would have taken time. These people must have suffered a lot."

The cop shook his head. "The cuts were done post mortem, thank God. These people were dead before they were disemboweled."

"What do you mean?"

"I mean they all died of asphyxiation and then were carved up. At least that's what the mortician is saying."

"At least they didn't suffer."

"You're telling me. Strangest thing though, and this might interest you, Priest, but it looks like some of their organs are missing, too. We can't be completely sure about that, but we've been collecting and counting and some stuff seems to be gone. Sounds like occult stuff, right?"

"It is odd," Niccolo agreed politely. "What can you tell us about the asphyxiation? Was a rope used?"

"Nope. No rope burns, no handprints, nothing. We found scratch marks on some of their necks, but they appear self-inflicted, like they were clawing at their own throats. It's like they suffocated but nothing was choking them. They just … couldn't breathe. It's like their trachea was squeezed from the inside. Really strange."

"That is strange."

"The mortician is thinking collapsed air pipes, but we aren't sure how that was achieved yet. He's going to run a full autopsy on each victim before we know anything for sure."

Arthur nodded. It didn't sound like something Jeremy did. If Jeremy was able to stop people from breathing like this, he would have done it to Arthur and Niccolo back at the shipyard. He wouldn't have needed to run away when things got dangerous.

Which meant it was the other child who was with him, Arthur decided. What power, though, could create something like that? Telekinetic? That was the likeliest suspect but he couldn't be sure.

"What else do you know about the cuts? Postmortem, right?" Niccolo asked.

"Yeah."

"Do they look like something a kid could have done, in your estimation?"

The officer looked at Niccolo like he was crazy. Arthur fought the urge to laugh. "Not unless that kid was as big an adult, strong as a horse, and a complete psychopath."

"Ah."

The cop turned back to Arthur, clearly unwilling to take Niccolo seriously anymore. "Whoever did this was butchering these people, not just cutting on them. No hesitation marks. The bodies were practically exsanguinated, though not in a clean way."

"Did anyone see anything?" Arthur asked. "Something like this, it seems like there would be witnesses or someone might have escaped. Was anything called in?"

"Nothing. We're canvassing the neighborhood but so far no witnesses have turned up. Most people were at work and the church is outside of town. We're hoping someone might have heard or saw something but I don't have high hopes."

"Alright," Arthur said, handing the guy a business card with his phone number on it. "If you find anything of use let me know."

The officer accepted the card and slid it into his pocket. "Sure thing."

Arthur headed back outside to the parking lot and Niccolo fell into step beside him. The priest was silent, brooding.

"No leads out of that," Arthur admitted. "I was hoping something would pan out."

"All of that devastation, and nothing to go on. A complete waste."

"That's not entirely true. It wasn't a complete waste. We know more now than we did before."

"What do you mean?"

"We know that the children are somewhere nearby, which is a huge step in the right direction. At least we know what part of Ohio to search. I'm going to get us a hotel here so we're in the area. They also hit this church instead of a different one."

"So?"

"So: why this church? There are bigger churches in the area, much more populated, so if the goal was to get national attention this wasn't a likely target. It must have some other significance, so we need to figure out what that is."

"Alright. Where do we go next?"

"I'm not sure yet, but I'm starting to think that Desiree might have been on to something. We need to do some research and find out why they picked here, and for now we have to keep our ears to the ground and be ready to move. My guess is Jeremy's next step is going to be putting those organs to use."

"He's harvesting and preparing for some seriously dark rituals. I just can't believe they could do something like this. They are only kids."

"Not 'they'," Arthur disagreed. "Both kids didn't have a hand in this. Only one. The officer was right, they wouldn't have been strong, nor cruel, enough to cut these people up."

"What do you mean?"

"Think about it: all of the people inside the church were given an almost peaceful death by asphyxiation before being butchered for their organs. Those two ideas don't really work together."

"So, you're saying that Jeremy did this behind the girl's back?"

"That's how it is seeming. Why give them a peaceful death if you're planning to do something brutal to their body right after? They must have been asphyxiated by the girl, because it also doesn't fit what we know about Jeremy. The organs were probably taken after, no doubt by one of Jeremy's allies."

"So you think Jeremy did this without her

knowledge?"

"Or her consent. That's my hope at least. I can't say for certain, but it is a likely possibility. I don't think she would have approved if she knew what he had planned."

"Then you don't think she's a fully willing participant."

"No. I don't."

"She still killed them," Niccolo argued.

"I know," Arthur replied, climbing into the driver's seat of the car. "But it's at least a small silver lining. Maybe there is hope for her redemption."

"Maybe," Niccolo agreed, though he didn't sound convinced.

It was a quiet trip north through Ohio to get back to Desiree, though this time Niccolo was less depressed and more introspective. He was thinking about their situation. If he wasn't brooding on what happened back at the shipyard Arthur was happy.

Arthur called Frieda again to give her an update once they made it back to his home. He made the call in the barn while Niccolo went inside the house to find Desiree and tell her what they saw.

Arthur filled Frieda in on the details of the Church of Saint Thomas. The bodies, the way they were sliced up, and the fact that most of it happened postmortem.

"Except for the priest," he explained. "He died horribly."

"You think Jeremy did it."

"I hope so. Would be pretty terrible to find out there's another player this late in the game."

Frieda let out a sigh. "You think that's his plan? To hit churches? Maybe we should warn the Vatican so they can put them on high alert."

"Would they want to? Hiring guards for the churches could be more damaging than just trying to withstand this attack."

"True."

"I don't think that's the plan anyway. This didn't feel like an ideal target or just an attack of opportunity. This feels like it is just the beginning."

"The beginning of what?"

"I don't know, but ... He's harvesting."

"Organs?"

"Mmhmm. I think he's planning to summon more demons. If I had to guess, he intends to rebuild the army they lost in Everett. With the number of organs he collected, he could be well on his way to achieving that. He could have a handful of demons already."

"Just keeps getting worse. You have to stop him, Arthur."

"I know."

"How is Niccolo?"

"Not great, but better," Arthur replied. "He's starting to come to terms with what happened, and keeping him busy is taking his mind off of his own problems."

"Is he going to get in the way?"

"I don't think so," Arthur replied. "I'm going to need his help, though. If Jeremy is indeed bringing in demons, then we're going to need an exorcist. I intend to save these people that Jeremy is possessing, not kill them."

"OK, Arthur, but don't do anything stupid. If Niccolo is becoming a liability then cut him loose before it is too late. Got it?"

"I will."

He thought to mention to Frieda about bringing

Desiree along, but quickly changed his mind.

"What's your plan?" she asked.

"They need supplies for a ritual of summoning, and there are only a few dealers in the region who could help them with something like that. I'm going to talk to Mitchell and see if he's heard anything. Hopefully I'll find out where the kids are staying and put a stop to all of this before anything happens."

"Do you think Mitchell will know?"

"I think he can find out."

"Alright. Keep me appraised."

"Will do. Stay safe."

"You too."

He hung up the phone and headed back across the driveway to the front door of his house. He steadied his breathing and pushed his emotions down. He was on a mission, which meant he didn't have time to let his emotions cloud his judgment.

It was time to face the piper.

***

Desiree and Niccolo were speaking quietly in the living room when Arthur opened the door and came inside, but they immediately stopped as he walked into the room. They turned and stared at him, concerned expressions on their faces.

"I'm not going to explode."

They exchanged glances. "We know that," Desiree said. "We're just wondering..."

"If I'll fall apart?"

This time they didn't answer. Arthur focused only on the kitchenette off to his right. His heart was pounding in his chest and his breath came in short gasps as the scent of home overwhelmed him. It smelled old and musty, uncared for, but the hints of hardwood were still there.

The floor of the kitchen was white linoleum, and it was impeccably clean now with no sign of the blood his family had spilled there. He saw them, though, in his mind's eye. He saw their lifeless bodies on the cold and unforgiving floor, staring up at the ceiling.

The emotional wave was intense and immediate, and he simply let it wash over him. The pain of loss threated to drown him, and he struggled to keep his head above it. Tears streamed down his cheeks, but he didn't care. All he saw were their bodies.

All he saw was his failure.

He had no idea how long he stood there staring at the linoleum, but he realized it was a lot of time when he suddenly felt a tap on his shoulder. He jolted back to reality and brushed away at the tears streaming down his cheeks.

"Arthur?" Niccolo asked, standing just behind him and to his left. "Are you alright?"

"I'm fine," he said, clearing his throat. "We need to get back on the road."

"Are you sure? We can take a minute—"

He shook his head. "We don't have time. Grab your things and let's move."

***

By the time they made it to Mitchell's shop it was evening. The sky was getting dark early here this time of year, but the days were starting to get longer. Arthur loved winter in Ohio, though he disliked the volatility of the weather.

Arthur hadn't seen his brother in months. He hadn't even talked to him on the phone in a couple of weeks. There was nothing to talk about, and they never called each other idly.

That was the thing about family: they didn't need to talk to each other to know that they were supported. His brother was a constant feature in his life, an anchor. He knew that Mitchell felt the same way.

Of course, it didn't help that Mitchell was also a stoner and useless much of the time.

"This is your brother's shop?" Desiree asked, clearly surprised as they pulled up to it. It was in an old strip mall that was mostly empty, especially at this time of day and while it was so cold outside. It had, in fact, been empty pretty much since Mitchell started peddling his wares to the occasional customer.

There were only two cars in the parking lot, and that counted the one they had driven. This wasn't a lull in the daily traffic, either: this was business as usual.

"Yeah," Arthur said. "This is his shop."

"It looks ..."

"Run down?"

"I wasn't going to say it like that, exactly."

"It's OK," Arthur said with a chuckle. "The store is more of a front business than anything else. Most of what Mitchell does is sell things to the Council, Church, and other collectors. He's a registered dealer for the Vatican, which means most of his business comes from people like me."

"Ah."

"He's also ... well ... uh ... you'll see."

Desiree raised an eyebrow at him, but she didn't say anything. Arthur pushed open the door and the first thing he noticed — the same as every other time he came here — was the smell.

Incense and smoke, but underneath was a strong hint of marijuana. A lot of it. That was the other reason Mitchell managed to stay in business, though Arthur was pretty sure he smoked more than he sold.

"Oh ..." Desiree said.

"Is that...?" Niccolo began to ask, but just then the beaded curtain to the backroom was pushed aside and Mitchell rushed into the room. He was a little bit bigger than Arthur, though of a similar build. The only difference was that he was flabby and a little more rounded.

"Sorry, I didn't know I had custo —"

He stopped midstream, eyes going wide when he saw his brother standing there between the other two; then, he grinned. He ran across the room and wrapped Arthur in a huge bear hug.

"Arty!"

"Mitchell," Arthur replied with a groan, barely able to breathe.

"What the heck are you doing here? This is a pleasant surprise."

"Not a social visit," Arthur said, gently extricating himself from his brother's embrace. "And we're on a tight schedule. I just need to know if you've heard anyone buying stuff that might be used in a summoning ritual in the last couple of days."

"That's pretty vague. There are a lot of summoning rituals."

"Black market stuff. Demons and organs."

Mitchell's expression soured. "I don't sell stuff like that."

"I know. But you know people who do. Look, Mitchell, I don't care and I'm not trying to bust any of your friends, I just need to know if you've heard anything strange in the last couple of days, especially if it involves kids."

"Kids?"

"Yeah. Kids."

Mitchell thought for a second. "No. Nothing that I can remember. But I can ask around if you want. Is this a part of what's been going on with the Church?"

"You've heard about that?"

"Everyone's heard about that. Lots of rumors, no details. Care to enlighten me?"

"Would that I could."

Mitchell shrugged. "Oh well. The rumors are more interesting anyway. People are freaking out. You need this information now?"

"Yeah."

"I'll make some calls. Feel free to make yourselves at home. Just don't break anything."

Then, he disappeared into the back room through the curtain of beads and out of sight. Arthur watched him go and then turned back to the other two with a shrug.

Desiree was eyeing the meager wares. "What is there to break?"

Arthur laughed. "Maybe his collection of glass pipes."

"Interesting guy," Niccolo offered.

"You have no idea."

They found some chairs in the corner of the room to sit down on. The shop was almost completely empty, the shelves barren except for a few random items scattered here and there. It was not the kind of place a normal person would likely take their wallet out the purchase things at. Mitchell had an incense display on the counter, but most of the incense was gone.

Mitchell took about an hour in the backroom before finally reappearing.

"Find anything?"

"A lot of stuff," Mitchell admitted. "Nothing in particular about items being sold, but my contacts are usually cagey with the details. I did hear something about an abandoned gas station that has been occupied for the last couple of months. Here's the kicker: a little girl has been hiding out there. Twice social services were called, but nothing ever came of it. Rumor has it, authorities steer clear of the place."

"You've got an address?"

"Of course."

"Thanks, Mitchell."

"No problem at all," Mitchell said, handing Arthur a slip of paper. "That's what brothers are for."

Chapter 7

Jeremy wasn't a huge fan of eating out at fast food restaurants, but there weren't a lot of other options in the area. Akron was turning out to be a pathetic and low-brow place to live. He had enjoyed his life in Everett eating at the Bishop's table, and his time spent in California was at least warm and comfortable.

Boy, was Ohio cold.

Miserably so. It wasn't even like there was snow or some other redeeming quality to the winter weather, just the cold wind that numbed his cheeks and made his eyes water. He hadn't really minded it when they first arrived, but it had since dropped nearly twenty degrees and stuck there.

Crappy food and cold winters: that was Ohio. He'd lived in Everett for a long time, so he knew cold weather, but at least he'd had an expensive manor to live in and expensive food to eat.

Fast food was all they had for every meal since he got to Ohio, and right now it was their dinner. He took a bite of his burger and chewed the cold beef slowly, wishing it was anything else.

Of course, he was the only one who seemed to have trouble with it. Megyn, on the opposite end of the spectrum, seemed to love it. It made sense when he thought about it: while she was living with the cultists in the service station they had eaten a lot of canned food. Eating out was a luxury. While Jeremy was enjoying fresh fruit in California or expensive dinners with Leopold in Washington, Megyn had been eating scraps.

The thought was somehow comforting.

She ate two whole sandwiches and all of her fries,

plus about half of his. Jeremy was morbidly fascinated at the disgusting way in which she gorged herself.

Of course, she wouldn't get to enjoy a lot of meals like this. Not unless they sped up their timeframe or found a way to make some extra money. Their budget wasn't going to last them much longer.

They were running low; they didn't even have enough money for another night in a hotel room. They were heading back to the service station now to sleep for the night. He hated the thought of staying in that dingy dump, but there weren't a lot of other options. They hadn't even cleaned up the bodies, which meant by now the place smelled.

He kicked himself for not taking anything off of the dead people back in the church. He'd been so wrapped up in the moment that he hadn't even thought about their money situation. He didn't want to let Megyn know that their funds were getting low, he just hoped that she would stop ordering so much damn food when they—

"Sir," the driver called out from the front seat. The car jerk to a stop and idled. They were almost back to the service station, maybe a quarter of a mile away.

Jeremy set his sandwich on the faux leather seat beside him and leaned forward to look through the front windshield at the roadway ahead.

He let out a gasp and narrowed his eyes. Parked in front of their home base was a vehicle that he recognized.

The priest's car.

The one the priest drove away from the shipyard after murdering his father.

"Bastards," he growled, reaching for the door handle.

"You shouldn't engage with them," the driver said, grabbing his arm to stop him. He had a fearful expression on his face.

"I'm not going to engage with them. I'm going to kill them."

"It's risky."

"It's my decision."

He shook his arm to free it, but the demon didn't release his grip.

"Let me go."

"I can't let you do this."

Jeremy attempted to extricate himself again, but still the demon held on. He was disgusted by such a cowardly demon. Leopold talked about the demons like they were a powerful force, subservient and loyal. All Jeremy learned about them was that they were just as weak as the humans they rode around in.

"I'm going to kill them. It isn't your decision."

"Your powers didn't work on the hunter before. You said so yourself."

"They worked well enough, and now Megyn is with me," he said, glowering at the demon. He could hardly believe that the creature was actually arguing with him. Its duty was to serve and act as a good little soldier.

Bishop Glasser would have never gotten such disrespect from the creature.

"It is too risky."

"I will decide if it is—"

"He's right," Megyn interrupted, speaking to Jeremy. "We should just leave. We stayed there too long anyway. Father told us we should always keep moving, but I didn't want to. It's my fault they are there."

"What about all of our stuff. Our supplies?"

"Our what?" Megyn asked.

Jeremy ignored her, focusing instead on the demon.

"It is in the trunk," the demon said. He let go of Jeremy's arm and put the car back into gear. "I've been keeping it close at hand in case something like this happened."

Jeremy was still furious and wanted nothing more than to charge into the service station and face the priest and his lackey head on. He wanted to kill the man so bad the rage made his eye twitch.

He didn't though, because it would be a waste of time. That was, at least, the rationality he used to calm himself down.

He was scared. Not of the priest: he'd already dominated him once, but of the hunter. Arthur somehow resisted his mental influence, and getting away was sheer luck.

Enemies weren't the only thing Leopold had in the region, and there was another stop he needed to make. An old alliance that the Bishop made, and one he could call upon in times of need.

This, he felt, was need enough.

"Fine. We'll deal with them another way."

***

He stayed that night in the cramped backseat alongside Megyn, though he didn't sleep much at all. It was cold and uncomfortable in the car and the wind howled outside. Megyn snored and tossed all night, making little moaning noises whenever she couldn't get comfortable. It was distracting and he didn't feel like he got any real rest at all.

They parked a few miles away from the service station on a backroad and Jeremy found himself wide awake and staring at the carpeted ceiling of the smelly car. He'd been hoping to begin his preparatory rituals the previous evening and get everything ready for the upcoming summoning event, but instead he found himself on the run once more.

He hated it. He hated being the one to run.

Not for much longer, he vowed. Soon, he would be the one doing the hunting.

He woke Megyn and the driver up early the next morning and got them back on the road before the sun came up. Their base of operations was lost to them now, but that mattered little. Right now it was important that they keep moving and keep their plans rolling. The sooner their agenda was finished the better.

They had allies in Ohio that they could call upon in a time of need, and those allies would be more than adequate for dealing with the ignorant priest and his hunter friend. He hadn't originally planned on reaching out to The Ninth Circle for help, but now it felt like a necessity.

***

"I don't like it here," Megyn whined, grabbing Jeremy by the coat as they walked up toward the junkyard entrance. She tried to pull him away, a concerned look on her face. "We should just go back."

"We can't," Jeremy replied, shaking his arm loose and shoving Megyn away. "These people owed our Father for what he did for them, which means that now they owe us."

"I'm scared."

Jeremy glowered at her. He couldn't stomach her constant simpering about everything, and he was annoyed that he had to bring her along. He would have left her in the car, but he had to admit that even he was a little bit afraid about meeting these people. Leopold had described them as ignorant savages, capable only of short sighted decisions.

Of course, part of him knew that he was so mad at Megyn because she was right. This place was creepy and more than a little bit intimidating. Endless piles of dead and rusty cars littered the surrounding area, stretching off in all directions. It felt like a graveyard of metal, rust, and decay.

If something went wrong, he would be glad to have Megyn at his side.

Nothing moved, and there was no sound in the area except for the wind. He expected to get rushed upon by a guard dog when they first walked up to the area — something he saw in countless movies — but the absence of even that made the place more eerie. He was starting to wonder if this was even the right place.

Still, he couldn't back down now: they no doubt already knew he was at the junkyard. They doubtless watched him already, so he refused to show weakness or fear. That was something the Bishop taught him, and he needed to show them that he meant business.

He must show them that he was the Bishop's rightful heir.

They walked through the graveyard of cars toward a small office building near the center. A group of three ugly men came out to meet them in front of it. They were dirty and disheveled and looked like they were probably inbred. Leopold hated working with them so many years ago, claiming that this was one of the dirtiest and weakest cells of the entire cult.

They were all underdressed for how cold it was outside. It was chilly and Jeremy saw his breath hanging in the air in front of him. One man wore overalls and a faded yellow shirt, and he seemed to be in charge of the others.

Another balding man was carrying a baseball bat and wearing overalls, and the last man was carrying a sawed off shotgun with rust on the barrel. Jeremy wasn't even sure if it would fire.

"Who're you?" yellow-shirt asked. He was chewing on something, and he turned and spat a wad of black tobacco juice into the dirt beside him.

Jeremy cleared his throat. "I am Jeremy Caldwell, and this is Megyn Wilford. We are the children and disciples of Bishop Leopold Glasser. Run along and tell your master that we are here."

The man eyed him for a long moment, chewing on the tobacco like a cow chewed cud. His face was leathery and cracked and he had a painful red rash covering the exposed skin on his arms.

He turned and spat another wad into the dirt.

"I don't know where you reckon you are at, boy, but we—"

"It wasn't a request," Jeremy cut in, keeping his voice steady. The man with the shotgun tensed up but Jeremy kept his focus on the leader. "I know what Leopold Glasser did for you and yours only a year ago when you murdered that man's family. Me and my sister are owed both sanctuary and assistance in our endeavors, and we're here to collect on our father's debt."

He tried to sound tough, but his voice was higher

pitched and less confident than he liked. Still, he pushed through knowing that he needed to put up a strong front.

Megyn was still clutching his arm, and she shivered beside him. Fear was the way in which the strong gave up their power to the weak. Jeremy had no intention of relinquishing any of his power. He forced his back to stay straight and looked the man in the eye.

A few minutes passed as the man sized them up, thinking. Finally, the man coughed, wiped his mouth, and then turned back toward the little decrepit shop the crew had walked out of.

"Come on then."

The other two men lowered their weapons, though they didn't look to happy about it. The guy with the bat, a skinny man with missing teeth and a weasel face, was leering at Megyn in a way that made Jeremy's skin crawl. He couldn't imagine the effect it was having on Megyn and hoped she hadn't noticed.

He was wondering if maybe they made a mistake in coming here. Maybe this was the wrong place and these weren't the people Bishop Glasser helped with information. Or maybe they wouldn't be willing to help and wanted to trick Megyn and Jeremy inside to try and hurt them.

If that was the case, then woe unto them for picking the wrong kids to try and fight. Still, he didn't like the way the men were looking at them.

They were led into the main room of the shop. It, too, was littered with broken and discarded trash. It smelled like a skunk had died in a backroom a few days ago and was just left there, but he was careful not to let it show on his face.

Three more cultists laid around inside the shop,

just as dirty and disgusting as the welcoming party, and they barely even perked up when everyone came in. A fan spun lazily overhead, though it did nothing except kick the dust around.

He had no idea why the fan was running, except maybe to dissipate the smell. It was cold in the building, maybe in the fifties and barely warmer than outside, though the gathered crew barely seemed to notice.

The tobacco chewer pointed at an empty and raggedy couch in the corner of the room.

"Wait dere," he slurred.

The couch was no doubt laced with insects, bed bugs, and other disgusting creatures he couldn't even imagine. Jeremy's skin crawled just thinking about it.

"I think we'd rather just wait..."

The man shot him a look that made clear this wasn't up for debate. Jeremy took Megyn's hand and dragged her over to the couch. He sat down, and then pulled her down next to him. She made a little moan as he did so, leaning forward and trying to touch the couch with as little of her butt as she could.

"We must be hospitable," he murmured.

Megyn didn't reply.

Yellow-shirt disappeared out the front door of the shop and back into the junkyard, leaving them alone with the rest of the crew of ugly and disfigured misfits. Jeremy struggled to remain calm, but he could feel them all staring at them. They were focusing on the two children like they were pieces of meat on offer.

Time passed; though it was impossible to tell how much. Maybe an hour, or it might have been only ten minutes. The place was quiet, the only sound people breathing and the occasional cough. It felt as though the two children were sitting inside a fishbowl or zoo. He couldn't be sure, but it seemed like the room was getting smaller.

"You're perty," one man said suddenly, breaking the silence. He pointed a crooked finger at Megyn and smiled at her with a mouthful of yellow teeth. "Bet ye smell good too."

"Jeremy…" she whispered, clutching his hand.

"We should leave," he decided. "Stay with me."

He began to stand up, but just then the door opened and two people came striding in. The first through the door was the yellow shirted leader who had brought them in. The second was, Jeremy figured, his master.

That man wore an expensive tailored and well-cut suit, his hair was trimmed and immaculate, and he was quite handsome with piercing eyes and angular features.

He glanced around the room, spotted Jeremy and Megyn on the couch, and then broke into a huge smile. It was a warm and friendly grin, and it filled Jeremy with relief.

"You must be Jeremy," the man exclaimed, rushing across the room. He took Jeremy's hand in his own and shook it gently, beaming down at them. "And Megyn, I presume? I've heard so much about both of you from my dear friend, Leopold. This is such a treat to finally meet you."

He said it with complete familiarity, though Jeremy was quite certain he'd never heard of this man before. He stood out, though Bishop Glasser never mentioned someone like him associated with this cell of the cult before.

"Yes. I'm Jeremy and this is my sister Megyn."

"It's so good to finally shake your hands. I am George Castinella. I was a dear friend of Leopold's, and it positively broke my heart to hear what happened to him. I can't imagine what you both must be going through. I'm so terribly sorry for your loss."

"How did you hear?"

George smiled, though this time it was less pleasant. "I hear many things. The world isn't as large as you might imagine."

"Well, thank you for your condolences," Jeremy muttered, standing up from the couch and brushing his clothes off. "That's actually why we are here, though. We were hoping you would honor—"

"You both must be starving," George cut in. He rudely snapped his fingers at one of the disgusting women off to the right to get her attention. "Fetch them some food."

"No, no, that is quite alright. We aren't hungry and—"

"Nonsense. It'll only be a moment to prepare something and Bertha is quite the chef."

Jeremy took a deep breath to steady his nerves.

"Thank you, then. Of course, we graciously accept."

"We should talk," George said, heading toward the exit. "Let's go for a walk, just the two of us."

Megyn grabbed Jeremy's hand in fear and flashed him a look of terror.

"Don't leave me here," she whispered.

"Megyn should come along as well. We are in this together."

"No," George replied. "Just us. You have my word, though, that no harm will come to either of you while you are here. You are my guests, and we would never dare to mistreat one of our own."

"We aren't cultists."

"But, you are family."

Jeremy hesitated. He didn't want to leave Megyn alone, but he also didn't want to pass up the opportunity to speak to George. He needed the man's help in dealing with the priest and hunter.

Plus, he knew Megyn could defend herself if the rest attacked her. It might even be good practice to help toughen her up a little bit.

"It'll only be a few minutes," he said, gently freeing his hand. "Just stay here."

"Jeremy."

"Stay."

Then, he turned and followed George out the door of the shop and into the sunny junkyard beyond. The cold hit him like a wall and he bundled his coat even tighter.

George was tall and regal and looked more like a businessman than a cult leader. There was something about him that just made him instantly trustworthy. Jeremy knew better than to trust that impression, though, and reminded himself that he had the upper hand here.

They walked for a few minutes through the piles of junk in silence before George finally spoke.

"I'm glad you came. I was worried that the Bishop hadn't told you about us and that you wouldn't seek us out after he was gone."

"He said you were friends and that you owed him."

"I owed Leopold a greater debt than I ever could have paid. He helped me damage and weaken our greatest enemy in ways we couldn't have dreamed of. I would have willingly done anything for him."

"That's actually why I am here. I was hoping that,

in that spirit, you might be willing to help us deal with a problem we've—"

"I think you should cancel your plans."

Jeremy stopped midstream, confused. "What?"

"I know you are trying to live out Leopold's mission for you. I heard about what the two of you did at the Church of Saint Thomas and I feel this is a misguided waste of your true potential."

Jeremy frowned. "How do you know that was us?"

George smiled at him and chuckled. "Coy. I like it. Leopold always said you were smart. That's why he trusted you so much."

"Then you also know that he never would have wanted us to stop living out his legacy. Even after we lost him. This was to be his greatest achievement. The shining pinnacle of his years of planning."

"Of course it was, but it was always a misguided agenda. The children he so painstakingly gathered are being rounded up all over the country even as we speak, and so far they've done very little to damage the Church or open the eyes of the world."

"Then more needs to be done. With what I have planned, no one will be able to dismiss us any longer. We will open the world's eyes."

"Absolutely, but not like this. Bloodshed and murder solve nothing. People can willfully disregard anything, even facts that are right before them. All that will come of this is you and Megyn will be caught, or worse, killed. If you are caught, you will be handed over to the church and your lives will be over."

"You're wrong."

"Leopold was wrong," George said. He stopped walking and shifted to face Jeremy. "He thought that this was the way to get things done, but this won't accomplish anything. This war you are trying to start...you've lost it before it's even begun. Your gifts, however, could be used to accomplish so much more. You could be the answer to all of our dreams."

Jeremy felt a burst of rage. "I won't stand here and listen to you speak ill of my father."

"Nor would I ever speak ill of him. Leopold was a great man, one of the greatest I've ever known. He was a visionary, Jeremy. What he did by gathering your family together was incredible: what he meant to do with it, however, was to waste all of your talents on a single-minded and unambitious plan. When last we spoke only a few weeks ago, I had finally convinced him of this. Alas, he died before we could finalize it."

"You what?"

"I convinced him that what he intended to do with this grand gesture was shortsighted and that there was a better way to use you children. He was going to call off the mission and together we were going to redirect the endeavor."

"You're lying."

"I would never lie. Not to you."

"He wouldn't have called it off. He wanted to activate all of us and start our attacks."

"He didn't, though, did he?"

"No, he was delaying until we gathered the next child."

"And he would have delayed again, and again. He postponed the agenda to go and collect another child, and it cost him his army and his family. He had no intention of activating any of you, though, after we spoke. You were his family, and he wasn't willing to take that next step and risk losing you."

"We were building an army."

"Of demons. That was to be your attack. We helped you build that army. We taught him the summoning rituals and gave him the names of the demons, and he knew that they were a better way. The demons were expendable, but the children were everything."

"You're lying."

"I'm not. When last we spoke we began forming new plans. He intended to gather one last child, Haatim Arison, and then together we would find a way to use all of the children to their fullest capabilities. We were ready to expand and take over the world."

Jeremy hesitated. It was true that the Bishop passed up multiple opportunities to begin his plan. He was in final stages of planning for years, in fact, but never actually gave the go ahead to begin.

Jeremy had known the Bishop's activation strategies for all of the children, which was how he'd sent out the commands for them to begin their attacks, but when last he spoke with Leopold the plan had been to wait.

Some of the children had clearly defined targets that the Bishop had chosen for them to maximize damage and visibility, but many more of the children had no clear idea of what they were supposed to do. The Bishop had never given them any real idea of how to do damage.

That didn't matter to Jeremy, though. The point was to have the children do something. They could all create some impact just by using their imaginations and powers. If nothing else, they would form a distraction to keep the Church busy until Jeremy had succeeded in his mission.

What George said about Leopold's unwillingness to begin rang of truth, however...

No, that couldn't have been true. If the Bishop was modifying his agenda, he would have told Jeremy. He told Jeremy everything about his plans, the mission, and what they were trying to accomplish.

Didn't he?

"You're lying. He had no intention of stopping. Once we had collected Haatim we were going to begin the attacks all across the country."

"Don't you get it, Jeremy? These attacks serve no purpose. Opening up the eyes of the public accomplishes nothing. The public can be lied to, manipulated, and trained to see things anyway we want them to. You were his chosen soldier, the one who helped him build his demonic army. You were the only one he needed."

"That's why it is my duty to honor his memory."

"Then honor his memory by succeeding in ways he could only dream of. Let me help you, and together we can truly wake the world up to your power."

"I intend to," Jeremy replied, frustrated. "That is why I need your help."

"Not like this. You aren't prepared yet and you only run the risk of getting yourself killed. All you are doing is squandering the Bishop's gifts."

Jeremy narrowed his eyes. "I am more than prepared. You saw what I did at the church. You know what I'm capable of."

"Are you prepared to lose everything?"

"Yes."

"To die, if need be?"

"Of course."

"To lose even Megyn?"

"If need be to accomplish the mission, then yes."

"Is Megyn equally prepared?"

"She is prepared to follow my lead."

"Is she prepared to die for you?"

Jeremy narrowed his eyes. "That isn't her decision to make."

"Isn't it, though?"

"If you speak to her of this without—"

"Relax," George interrupted, "I have no intention of speaking to Megyn about anything. Your relationship with her is your own, and what details you choose to give her are yours to decide."

"Good."

"What I am saying is this: if you choose to go through with this plan, I will support you, but give me the opportunity to show you a better way."

Jeremy hesitated. "I'm listening."

"How long has it been since you saw your father? Or your mother? Don't you miss them? Don't you wish for a normal life?"

"Of course I miss them, but it means nothing. I'm not meant for a normal life. None of us are."

George pressed on, ignoring his protestation. "If you do things right then you can have both. You could have a family, a normal life, and still accomplish the mission you've set yourself upon. I can teach you how."

"That involves cancelling my mission. I can't do that. I've already collected the items I need and I'm ready to finalize this."

"You plan to hit the hospital, don't you?"

Jeremy was shocked. "How do you know that?"

"I told you: I knew Leopold, and I know you. Together, we can do so much more."

Jeremy shook his head slowly. The conversation was turning in directions he didn't want it to go. He had to reassert himself.

"I don't need you to teach me anything," Jeremy replied. "I need for you to honor the contract you made with my father. You already said you would."

"Of course I will, but there is more we could—"

"There are two people after us, a hunter and the priest who killed my father. The hunter is Arthur, and he was your mistake. You murdered his family with the Bishop's help, so now you need to help fix the mess you made."

"Arthur shouldn't still be alive," George said. "A miscalculation, I admit, and one I fully intend to rectify."

"Well, he is. I want you to have your little minions in there deal with them, and that is all I want from you."

"I understand what you want to achieve but—"

"Will you help me or not?" Jeremy asked, furious. "I don't care at all about your plans or your agenda. I don't care about anything you have to say about Leopold or any of this. I don't need your opinion, I need your help. All I want to know is: will you do as I ask and help us, or am I wasting my time?"

He did his best to make the last sound like a threat. A long moment passed while George weighed what Jeremy had said. He was frowning, clearly unhappy with the turn the conversation had taken, but Jeremy didn't really care.

He didn't like that the man was disparaging Leopold's agenda. How dare he assume that he knew better than the Bishop?

"Fine," George said finally. "I owe your father, and so I owe you."

"Really?"

"We will take care of the hunter and the priest for you. One of my friends has told me where they are staying in the city and I will send my men there. We will respect the contract we made with your father, even though your mission is misguided."

"Excellent."

George frowned at him. "You could have had everything. Maybe you still can. I want you to understand that my door is always open for you and for Megyn. Should you change your mind, just know that I will be here waiting and ready to help you achieve so much more."

"That won't be necessary," Jeremy said.

He cheered internally, realizing that he had won. They would do his bidding, and he was getting exactly what he asked for.

He turned and began walking back through the junkyard toward shop to gather up Megyn and get the heck out of here. Hopefully the food wasn't ready yet and he could beg out of eating it ... or maybe just take some to go and throw it away. He might be poor and hungry, but he had standards.

He had no desire to stick around with these dirty and creepy cultists for a moment longer than he needed to.

He stopped, though, and turned back to face George.

"You're wrong."

"Oh?"

"Leopold was a great man, and his plan was perfect. We will get him the justice he deserves and punish everyone who ever spoke ill of him."

Including you, he thought, but didn't add.

George narrowed his eyes, clearly aware of the unspoken threat in the words.

"Careful, boy. Remember who you are speaking

with."

"I could say the same."

George stared at him and Jeremy only smiled.

"We will win."

"I hope so, young man," George said, turning away from Jeremy and walking deeper into the junkyard. He called to Jeremy over his shoulder without looking back, "for your sake."

Chapter 8

"Jeremy isn't coming back," Arthur said, laying his head back on the headrest of his rental car and frowning. He was exhausted and cold from staying up all night in the car. They couldn't run the engine, and the blankets they had taken from the hotel room to keep them warm weren't enough to fight off the chill overnight.

Niccolo nodded from the passenger seat beside him and let out a sigh. "I didn't expect they would. Do you think they saw us?"

"I'm assuming they spotted us yesterday when we first got here. Or, they must have had someone watching the place to warn them not to return."

"What do we do now?"

Arthur wasn't completely sure. Mitchell had given them this location, and it had panned out perfectly. The children had been here, and the little girl might have been living here for several days or weeks. Maybe months even, just like Mitchell had said.

The stakeout hadn't panned out. They had been so close to catching Jeremy and yet now it was just another dead end. That's how it went sometimes, Arthur knew. They would get another chance to catch him, they just had to hope it didn't come too late.

"Let's completely search the place," Arthur said, finally. "Might find a clue we missed or somewhere we should go next."

They climbed out of the car and headed over to the broken service station across the street. Arthur had parked out of sight the previous day when they arrived, but it was impossible to hide it completely and still see the building.

They had staked the building out over the long night, and it had been miserable. Desiree had opted not to come with them out here, which turned out to have been the better choice. She was in her hotel bed, nice and toasty, while they were freezing in the car.

To his credit, Niccolo hadn't complained about how cold it got in the car, but he did fall asleep a couple of times.

The pumps had been torn out years earlier and the fuel reservoir filled with cement. This place was waiting for a demolition crew that was never coming. At least not until gentrification or some other external force made the land worthwhile.

The smell of rot, and of human flesh rotting in the heat, wafted out of the interior and overwhelmed his senses as they walked up to the door.

Niccolo gagged next to him. "What is that?"

"You should wait out here."

"Why, what is it?"

"More death."

Niccolo pursed his lips, but he didn't take Arthur's advice. He followed into the room behind Arthur, and into the carnage and devastation of the rundown gas station.

Three bodies were lying on the floor, each in various stages of dismemberment. It hadn't been long since they had been killed, around the same time as what happened in the church by Arthur's estimation. The cuts weren't precise; they were made by an unpracticed hand.

"Who are they?" Niccolo breathed.

"Hard to tell," Arthur said. "Vagabonds, maybe."

"Why kill them? Do you think they stumbled onto the place looking for somewhere to get out of the cold?"

"Possibly. Look closer," Arthur said, walking over to the bodies and waving his hand over the midsection of one. "The organs are missing, just like at the church."

"You said they had everything else they need for a summoning ritual, right?"

"It looks like he's harvesting many people. Whatever he's planning, it's big. He must be bringing quite a few demons into the world."

"We need to notify the Vatican."

"We will," Arthur said. "But in the meantime, we still have to find Jeremy and stop him."

"I think...I'll wait outside."

"Suit yourself."

Niccolo made the sign of the cross over his chest, turning away from Arthur and heading back outside. Arthur searched for any clues about where Jeremy and the little girl went next.

More people had been living here than just the little girl. At least two or three other people, the same ones that had been butchered in the main room.

Why kill them, though? If they were allies of the Bishop, then why would Jeremy want them dead?

He was solidifying his influence over the little girl. She wasn't a fully willing participant, then his best course of action would be to get her out on an island. Once he was the only person she could turn to, then she would be willing to do anything he asked of her.

Even though he found some more clues about their circumstances, nothing in the building made it clear where they went after leaving the service station. No addresses, names, nothing of value that they could use to track the children down. Arthur left with more questions than answers.

What was Jeremy planning to do with all of the organs? How many demons could he possibly summon? Everyone he had killed so far felt orchestrated, like he was building up to something much bigger.

What, though? The church, and now this … what was Jeremy's end game?

He finally headed back out into the cold and found Niccolo waiting outside. Niccolo was on his cellphone, speaking with the Vatican. He couldn't overhear anything, but the call wasn't going well. Niccolo scowled and touched his chin, something he did whenever he was frustrated.

Arthur waited until the call was over before speaking. Niccolo hung up and then shook his head.

"They aren't interested?"

"They are, but there's nothing they can do to help right now. It'll take at least two days to get us any help."

"By then it will be too late."

"That's what I said. They just told me to deal with it."

"Sounds like they have faith in you."

"They shouldn't. Look how things went down in California."

"If it wasn't for what you did, Bishop Glasser would be on the other side of the world terrorizing even more people."

Niccolo shook his head and waved his hand. "We need to hurry. Jeremy still has a head start on us and we're no closer to stopping him. We're always one step behind."

"We need to know where to search before we start hurrying," Arthur argued. "You're right that we're consistently one step behind, but rushing around isn't going to bridge that gap."

"So, what then?"

"We find Jeremy's next target. The church was an intentionally chosen location, so we know the next attack will also be important."

"How do we figure that out?"

"More research. I need you to call your friends at the Vatican or a local office and find out every place the Bishop might have served at while he was in Ohio. Desiree is going to the Akron library to search for information, and with luck she'll turn something up. We need to look up any location that might be useful and check it out. If we know who in Ohio the Bishop considered an enemy, then we know who Jeremy's next target is going to be."

"Alright," Niccolo said. "But, what if we don't find anything?"

Arthur didn't answer. If they didn't find a location of the target before the attack, he knew, then they would sure as hell find it afterwards.

Chapter 9

Mikael still hadn't called them, and they had been out here in Minnesota for two days waiting for something to change. Frieda found herself constantly bored and more than a little annoyed by the lack of action. If he was one of her hunters, she would already be considering punishments for his inability to complete this job.

He wasn't, though. All she could do was stew, and it drained on her patience. Frieda enjoyed being in charge, and she hadn't realized how much she enjoyed it until someone else had the power.

Worse, Mikael enjoyed reminding her that he oversaw this situation whenever they spoke. He would tell her time and again that he was the one running the show and she was simply here as a favor for the Church. Anytime Frieda questioned the way he was handling this case that was the first thing he brought up.

Handling, in fact, was too strong of a word. All she and Abigail had been doing since they arrived was sitting around and waiting for something to happen. They spent most of their time in the hotel room with bad television shows waiting for Mikael to tell them it was time to move.

Which was an utter waste of resources as far as she was concerned. Other hunters needed their help, particularly Arthur's situation out in Ohio. Based on his last check in, something major was happening. He hadn't yet tracked Jeremy down, and she could sympathize: she'd thought that threat was dealt with when the Bishop was killed.

The idea of possibly dozens of demons running around Ohio because of Jeremy was certainly worse than whatever was happening out here with Curtis and Mikael.

She finished her current phone call with Garfield, slid the phone back into her pocket, and then tossed a sock over at Abigail. Abi was sitting on the hotel bed with a bowl of cereal on her lap and she scowled at Frieda when the sock almost landed in her bowl. She had milk stains all over her shirt and was too engrossed in the television to care.

"What was that for?"

"Why is your sock on my chair?"

"That's where it wants to be," Abigail said, throwing the sock back. "It's the sock's home."

"Sure," Frieda replied, pushing the sock onto the floor. "If only we had a bag the sock could go in."

Abigail turned back to her shows. "If only," she agreed.

This would be the only time of the day when Abigail wouldn't complain about being bored. Once she ran out of cartoons in her morning programming it would be game on for keeping the little girl occupied and out of her hair.

"What's Arthur doing now?"

Frieda hesitated for a moment, caught off-guard by Abigail's question. She wasn't sure how much of the truth she should admit. On the one hand, Abigail had experienced the worst that this world had to offer, being abused and tortured by a cult for many months — maybe even years, it was impossible to tell — before Arthur finally rescued her.

But, on the other hand, she was still just a kid and didn't really deserve to be overwhelmed with things like this. Frieda wouldn't hide the truth of her work from Abigail, but she didn't want the girl to grow up thinking the world was only full of bad people.

"He's helping to track down a target for me."

"More of the kids?"

"Yes."

"Kids like me?"

"Not quite," Frieda said. "These children were taken in by someone evil and taught to do bad things."

"So ... exactly like me?"

Frieda laughed. "Shut up and go brush your teeth."

"Again?" Abigail asked, scrunching up her face.

"Once after each meal. You finished your cereal, right?"

"Yep."

"Then brush your teeth. You know the rules."

Abigail groaned, climbing slowly from the bed. "I'll go brush my teeth if you take me to see a movie."

"This isn't a negotiation."

Abigail shrugged. "Do we have a deal?"

"No, we don't have a deal," Frieda said, laughing. "But, I'll think about it. Now get your butt in there and brush your teeth."

Abigail grumbled some more under her breath as she headed to the bathroom. She slammed the door behind her, and a second later Abigail heard the sink turning on.

"Arthur doesn't stand a chance," Frieda whispered, smiling to herself.

Soon she would tell him that he was Abigail's guardian. After this mission once the children were dealt with. The expression on his face would be priceless, especially once he figured out that she was a handful.

It was imperative that he locate Jeremy and bring him back to the Church. By all reports, Jeremy was the closest of the Bishop's advisors and in on his plan, so if anyone could put an end to this before more children were hurt, it was him.

Her phone rang.

"Hello?"

"Tolson's Bakery. One hour."

It took her a second to recognize the voice on the other end of the line, but Mikael hung up before she could respond. The line went dead and she cursed for being so slow to respond.

She went over and banged on the bathroom door.

"Come on, Abi. We need to get on the road."

Abigail poked her head out of the bathroom, still brushing her teeth. When she spoke, the word was garbled.

"Now?"

"No, tomorrow," Frieda said sarcastically. "Yes now. Let's go. Move, move, move."

Abigail disappeared back into the bathroom for another minute before rushing back out. She quickly changed her shirt and then together they headed out of the hotel room and downstairs toward the lobby.

"Where are we going?"

"Tolson's Bakery."

Abigail frowned. "What? Why?"

"No clue. That's where Mikael said to meet him."

Abigail was silent for a minute. They went out of the lobby into to the parking lot and the cold air washed over them. Abigail made a noise and pulled her coat tighter, using the collar to block her face.

"Why did you have to pick a job that was somewhere so cold?"

Frieda chuckled as they climbed into the car and got on the road. Adrenaline coursed through her veins as well as a little bit of nervousness. No matter how many times she told herself this would be an easy cake-walk mission, she couldn't tamp down her excitement.

They arrived at the bakery with about twenty minutes to spare. She pulled to a stop in an alley that overlooked the bakery and then parked.

A minute passed.

"So ... now what?" Abigail asked.

"No clue," Frieda said.

"Can you turn the heat on?"

"I don't want to waste the gas."

Abigail mumbled something under her breath. Frieda ignored her. She stayed in the car until they heard from Mikael.

"He didn't tell you why we were coming here?"

"He didn't tell me anything. He just said the bakery and an hour and then hung up."

"Oh."

Another minute passed in silence.

"You didn't think to ask him why?"

"He didn't give me the chance. I told you, he just hung up."

"Mmhmm."

"Mmhmm, what?"

"Maybe you were too slow in responding."

"It was right away. First, he said the bakery's name and then he immediately hung up. I couldn't have possibly responded."

"Sure."

"Sure?"

"Maybe his phone died."

"I doubt it. Some people just do that."

"Yeah," Abigail said. "Like you?"

"That's different."

"Oh."

Another few minutes of silence. Frieda rubbed her hands together as the cold air seeped into the car.

"So ... we're just waiting for him to get here?"

"Yeah."

"Why not inside?'

"You ask a lot of questions," Frieda said.

"You don't have many answers, though."

"One would think you'd stop asking."

"Just trying to get the facts."

"Mmhmm."

The back-right door of the car suddenly opened up, letting in a strong gust of wind, and someone climbed in. Frieda panicked. She shifted in her seat, grabbing the grip of the pistol tucked in her waistband and pulling at it. It got caught on her coat pocket, and it took her an extra couple of seconds to shake it loose.

Enough time that if the person in the backseat of her car wanted them dead, they would be. Gun free, she spun in the seat and leveled it at the man in the back.

Sitting in the back seat was Mikael, a bemused expression on his face as she struggled.

"Would you like some help?" he asked, tone devoid of all sarcasm. If anything, that made the verbal jab worse.

"You scared the crap out of me," Frieda said, sheepishly sliding her gun away.

"I can see that."

"Proving a point?"

"Whatever do you mean?"

"Why are we here?"

"Every day, like clockwork, our target comes here for lunch."

"So, you think this is a good place to grab him?"

"This is a good place to show you something," the man corrected. "You were wrong: Curtis is dangerous."

Frieda sighed. "He isn't dangerous, though. He's only an empath. He can read emotions by touching people, but little else."

"Watch."

He pointed over her shoulder toward the small bakery across the street. Tolson's was also a restaurant, and the place was getting busy with the lunch hour rush. They mostly did cold sandwiches, though, which she didn't much care for.

"What am I watching for?"

Mikael didn't answer. A few seconds passed and then Curtis walked up the sidewalk from the south. He weaved around pedestrians and then headed right into the bakery.

Curtis went up to the counter, and the man working there greeted him with a huge smile. They talked for a second, the kid passed over a couple of bills, and then he went off to find a seat.

"He bought food," Frieda said dryly. "Is that what you wanted me to see?"

"Watch closer."

She sighed. Curtis was very friendly, talking to various patrons in the restaurant. He touched them on the shoulders and arms and shook a lot of hands. It was as a politician moving through the crowd.

"He's outgoing. So what?"

The man sighed. "I can't make it any clearer. You said he's an empath and can read emotions. Clearly, he can also implant them."

"What?"

"He is creating happiness in these people for his own uses."

Frieda wasn't convinced. "Just because he's talkative doesn't mean he can create feelings in people. Maybe he's just reading them to get a sense of their mood. Knowing that could help him know how to navigate conversations with them."

"No. I thought so as well the first few times a saw it, but it is too consistent, and he does it regularly. Every day he comes here for lunch and he always gets discounts on his meal. Then he goes to various other places of business and creates similar effects on the proprietors for different purposes. He's dangerous."

Frieda hesitated. "Maybe he can enhance someone's emotions. But that doesn't change our mission. We still have to bring him in."

"No. I agree: it doesn't change anything. It just means we need to tread carefully when we move in to apprehend him."

"We could grab him right now," Frieda offered. "We're already here."

"It is too risky and there are too many people around."

Frieda paused. "What if he kills someone?"

"He won't."

"You can't know that for certain."

"He's made no indication that such would be his intent."

"What if there is no indication until he actually does it? If he kills someone, and we could have stopped him today and didn't, then we are responsible for it."

"You're argument is flawed."

"How so?"

"What if by doing as you want and grabbing him we provoke him into killing someone? If we go in while we are unprepared and lacking intelligence on the situation, we could spark this innocent boy to act out in a dangerous fashion he might not otherwise have. Then, such a decision and its consequences would likewise be upon us."

"What would he do? He's an empath. By your own admission the worst he could do is plant depressive emotions in someone. Making someone sad isn't dangerous."

"Sad enough to commit suicide?"

"Not likely."

"Not impossible, either. Until we know more, we cannot take the risk of confronting him. We will continue to monitor until we are prepared to deal with him."

"How long will that be?"

"Until I say otherwise."

"So, you brought us out here just to say we aren't going to do anything today?"

"I brought you here to show you this because I was worried you would do something rash and thereby jeopardize the mission."

"Fine. We will keep watching and waiting. We won't do anything."

"Good."

She turned her car back on, letting the heat wash over here. "We're going back to our hotel. You'd best get out unless you want to come along for a ride."

"No, thank you."

He opened the rear door and slid back out into the cold, and she immediately pulled back onto the roadway. Inside the diner, Curtis was still finishing his lunch, talking to a few people. He had a crowd around him, excited and happy.

It wasn't too crazy of an occurrence to have happy

people around an enigmatic teenage kid, but there was some truth in what Mikael had told them. It was possible that Curtis could implant emotions.

So what? That didn't change their mission. She didn't even think it increased their risk. He couldn't throw cars or destroy minds the way some of the more dangerous children could.

Arthur could be brash and impatient, and he made a lot of mistakes, but at least he didn't sit back and second-guess himself at every turn. Curtis would have been caught and handed over to the church by now.

Or, maybe dead.

That was the old Arthur though. He used to be cold and heartless, a dog on a chain that she could set loose against their enemies. All of that culminated in West Virginia when he murdered those cultists. That had terrified her in ways she had never even imagined. She experienced a lot of dark and twisted things in her life, but when Arthur killed those people she saw a side of him she'd never even imagined.

That anger and brutality...

Then, he had changed. He saw the world in a new light and interact with everything differently. He had gone from a heartless killer to something else.

Frieda would never admit it to him, but when he first suggested adopting Abigail after West Virginia, she had been the one to raise objections to the Council and stop the adoption. She thought it was to replace the daughter he had lost back in Ohio, and that a broken man like him had no place raising a child.

But, over the last few months, and particularly the last few weeks, he had shown himself to be a changed man. He had sworn off killing, and she prayed his newfound mercy would last.

She also prayed, however, that it wouldn't get him killed.

In their world, however, that was a nearly impossible tradeoff: demons and other horrors that inhabited their nightmares didn't know mercy.

Chapter 10

Niccolo settled back into the ugly yellow arm chair in their cheap hotel room just inside of Akron. Outside the window was the brown and unforgiving landscape of Ohio in winter. It was doubtless quite beautiful in the spring, but in the bleak winter it was entirely uninviting.

He was exhausted and rundown by their lack of progress. Jeremy was a murderer, and even at fifteen years old he was willing to commit atrocities in the name of his misguided beliefs. What would he be capable of when he was an adult? He had been indoctrinated by Leopold Glasser to do horrible things.

The reason it was so hard for Niccolo to come to terms with what Jeremy had become was because they might not be able to save him. Niccolo had spent his entire life with one unshakable belief: no one was beyond salvation.

Yet, what Jeremy had done went beyond the pale, and he was wholly unrepentant in his actions. Even if Jeremy fell to his knees and begged for forgiveness, he wouldn't deserve it.

If Jeremy was beyond redemption, then so was Niccolo.

He had murdered a Bishop. That, alone, was a fact that he could live with. After all, the Bishop had given him no other choice: one of them was going to die.

The problem, however, was that part of him was relieved by it. The Bishop died, and with him went the threat of everything he stood for. That was the reason Niccolo knew he was beyond redemption.

Part of Niccolo was happy with what he'd done.

The irony was that Arthur didn't even know the

true extent of Niccolo's flaws: Arthur thought Niccolo's depression stemmed from the murder, not the intent. He saw pity in the Hunter's eyes every time they were together.

Such pity was entirely misplaced: Niccolo wasn't ashamed of what he had done, he was ashamed of who he had become. Or, it was who he always was. He was a murderer and he had enjoyed taking the man's life.

Circumstances, context, they meant nothing when weighed against the value of his soul. With such a consideration, Niccolo fell far short of salvation.

He wasn't giving up on life or his service to the church. He still had a duty to the faith, and further a duty to the human race. He had taken on this burden when he joined Arthur in hunting the Bishop down, and he would see it through to the end before he returned to the Vatican to confess his crimes and receive his punishment.

Even with the Bishop dead, though the struggle wasn't over with: Jeremy was still a danger to everything that the church stood for. He was powerful, too, and capturing him would be difficult. Arthur worried about that, though the man didn't admit as much aloud.

"Penny for your thoughts?" Arthur asked suddenly.

The voice startled Niccolo and he jumped a little bit in his chair. He had been so wrapped up in his mind that he'd forgotten Arthur was even there.

Arthur was lying on the bed and staring up at the ceiling. His legs hung over the side and he had his fingers folded across his chest.

Desiree was at the local Akron library searching for any references to the Bishop's storied history in this town. She hadn't found anything back in Athens, Ohio, but now that they had a cleaner idea of where to look she was making more progress. They had narrowed the search region, now scanning through countless news articles going back dozens of years.

Thus far, she had determined that he had been here and she found links to him serving over Saint Thomas Church some forty years earlier. She was incredibly good at research and kept meticulous notes. Niccolo was very impressed and glad to have her along helping them out. He would have been out at the church assisting her, but right now was no good to anyone. He was simply too distracted.

"Nothing in particular."

"Really? You seemed pretty focused there for a minute."

"Nothing I can fix," Niccolo corrected, shifting in the chair. "I can't get my mind to relax for even a moment, but the thoughts do no good. I feel like I'm just spinning my wheels."

"Thinking about the shipyard?"

"Constantly."

That moment haunted him whenever he closed his eyes: Leopold's face, shredded and bloody from where Niccolo had shot him. He was lying on the floor and Niccolo stood over him with a gun. All he saw was that moment.

The moment when Niccolo had murdered him.

"It wasn't your fault," Arthur continued. "There was no other choice."

"There is always another choice."

"That other choice would have been for you to die instead of him. How could that have been better?"

"There could have been another way. A way in which neither of us died."

"Maybe," Arthur conceded. "But, maybe not. Thinking about 'what if' scenarios for that moment isn't going to do you any good. All we can do now is focus on what comes next."

"What does come next?" Niccolo asked. He genuinely wanted to know, because right now he couldn't see any future where he moved forward with what he'd done. "I'm a murderer. That is an unforgivable crime. There is no redemption for that. I am beyond God's love."

"Nothing is beyond forgiveness."

"Not for a murderer, and certainly not for a priest-turned-murderer. What I did was wholly and absolutely unforgivable."

"Life doesn't exist in absolutes," Arthur argued. "What if we had let Leopold escape? What if we weren't able to catch him or bring him to justice? What if he was able to continue kidnapping Vatican Children and enacting his agenda? Think of all of the children who would still suffer because of your inaction."

"I didn't say stopping him wasn't the right thing to do. I said that my choice of how to stop him makes me a killer."

Arthur was quiet for a long minute, before finally continuing. "Have you ever read the Bhagavad Gita?"

"No."

"In it, a soldier attempts to throw down his weapons and do his duty as a soldier because doing so meant he would have to kill people and he knew it was unforgivable. However, his God tells him that he must fight because it is his duty and purpose in life to be a soldier, and such duty outweighs the impetus of his religion not to kill."

"I'm not Hindu. Last I checked, neither were you?"

"That isn't the point," Arthur said. "It isn't about religion or theology, it's about the lesson in the story. My point is that your duty is what matters. Let's say in this argument you are right. Let's say that in killing the Bishop you have damned yourself to an eternity in hell, but, by killing him you saved the lives of many people, including children. Would you still do it?"

Niccolo hesitated. "My duty wasn't to kill him, it was to bring him in."

"We tried that. We did our best and everything we could and it still wasn't enough to bring him in alive. There was no other recourse than to murder him. So, would you take it back and let the Bishop walk free if it meant your soul was safe?"

Niccolo rubbed his hands across his face and shook his head. "I don't know."

"Yes, you do," Arthur said. "Just like I do every single time I take a life. I don't enjoy killing people, but if it needs to be done I also don't hate myself for it. I can't imagine for one second that you would put your own life above those of the children the Bishop was terrorizing and manipulating."

"Maybe..."

"It isn't in you to just let other people suffer so that your life is easier. If that was the case, you never would have become a priest, nor an exorcist, and you sure as hell wouldn't have come with me to hunt the Bishop at that shipyard."

"And, maybe that is the problem. Maybe the fact that we can sit here in this hotel and justify murdering someone is why we will never be allowed redemption. Maybe you're right and there was no other way. But, maybe you're wrong, too."

"I'm wrong about a lot of things, but this isn't one

of them. You've stepped out of your cozy life and into another world, and you have a purpose now that extends beyond your ten commandments or your simple life as a Vatican priest. You have a duty to protect the unprotected and defend the innocent. If you're going to get caught up on little details each time—"

"Someone is coming," Niccolo interrupted, leaning forward in his chair and squinting out the window. It was gray and foggy outside, but he was certain that his eyes weren't deceiving him.

Two men had gotten out of a car and were walking toward the entrance to the hotel. Both were carrying shotguns.

"What?"

Arthur jumped quickly off the bed and rushed over to the window to stand next to him. Niccolo pointed down toward where they were coming.

"Two men," Niccolo replied. "Both armed."

Arthur frowned. "Where there are two, there are probably more."

"What do you mean?"

Arthur walked over to the bedside table and grabbed his tranquilizer gun. "They will be coming from a few different directions and up both stairwells, hoping to corner us."

"Who?"

"The Ninth Circle, if I'm guessing. Impossible to know for certain. I wonder how they found us."

Niccolo felt a chill run down his spine. "You don't think...? You think they are here for us?"

"I know they are. It doesn't matter. We need to get moving."

Niccolo stood up from the chair. He jolted in

surprise and almost dove to the floor when something hit him and bounced to the floor.

"Heads up," Arthur said.

Niccolo picked the item up off the floor: it was his duffel bag, and it was empty. He dumped it out on the floor earlier to go through his clothing, an action he regretted now.

"Thirty seconds," Arthur said. "Grab what you can, because we aren't coming back."

Then, Arthur headed over to the door of their hotel room and gently opened it. Niccolo rushed over to his pile of clothes and frantically scooped them into the duffel bag.

He got most of the clothing inside and zipped it when he heard a low whistle. Arthur gestured at him to come.

Arthur held up his tranquilizer gun and made a shushing motion with his finger over his lips. Then, he pointed across the hallway. Another hotel room door stood open across from them, and it was empty inside.

"Go," Arthur mouthed. Niccolo didn't hesitate, just went.

Arthur followed Niccolo across the hallway and into the other room, closing both doors behind them. Then, he made his way over to the window overlooking the parking lot outside. This one was at the opposite side of the hotel.

"Two cars," Arthur whispered, scanning the parking lot. More people were milling around outside. "Maybe a third."

"Whose room is this?'"

"No one," Arthur said absently. "I picked the lock."

"What if it had been occupied?"

"It wasn't. Besides, we're only going to be here for

a minute or two.”

“That isn’t the point.”

Arthur ignored him. “Two cars on this side and one out back means at least six people, probably eight. They’re going to have a few guarding the exits and the rest tightening a noose around us.”

“What do we do?”

“We need to get out of here,” Arthur said. “We’re parked on the side of the hotel, and there’s no stairwell over there so hopefully there’s no guard either.”

“Alright.”

Arthur held up his tranquilizer gun and frowned at it. He drew the revolver from the small of his back and held it up.

“They might be demons.”

“And they might not be,” Niccolo argued, grabbing his revolver and pushing it down. “We have no way of knowing for sure, but I don’t think we should jump to using a weapon that might kill them on a hunch.”

Arthur opened his mouth to object and then changed his mind. With a sigh, he slid the revolver away and hefted the tranquilizer gun instead.

“Fine. Stay behind me, and move fast. We aren’t going to have a lot of time to get out of here once they spot us, so if I start running you best keep up.”

Niccolo stayed extra close to Arthur as they headed for the exit of this unoccupied hotel room. Arthur motioned for Niccolo to be still and then leaned close to the peephole that peered out into the hallway.

Niccolo heard some people talking on the other side of the door. He craned his neck to listen but heard little.

A second later, and there was a huge crashing sound from across the hallway. He jumped a little bit at the sudden noise, and Arthur grabbed his arm, steadying him. Someone had just busted their door open, and he heard a flurry of footsteps as the cultists stormed into their room.

"They aren't here," someone shouted.

"Check the exits."

"You, stay here."

The footsteps of several men rushed down the hallway in opposite directions, disappearing back down the stairs. He mouthed the words 'one more' to Niccolo and held up his gun.

Niccolo nodded and sucked in a steadying breath. He could do this: he'd been in firefights before. He wished like hell that he'd gone to the restroom earlier and prayed his bladder didn't get the best of him.

Arthur turned the handle and threw the door open. Niccolo saw a surprised guard in the doorway of their hotel room. He was holding a shotgun in his right hand, but right now it was resting down at his side.

The man spun when he heard the opposing door open, but too slowly. Arthur already had his tranquilizer gun up and he fired off a dart.

It hit the man squarely in the neck, and he reached up for it like grabbing a mosquito. Arthur rushed forward, using his free hand to catch the man's raggedy t-shirt and lower him to the floor.

He nodded toward the stairwell. "Stay low," he whispered.

Niccolo nodded. He rubbed his sweaty hands on his pants and drew his own tranquilizer gun. Slowly, they crept through the hallway to the stairs that led down to the lobby. Niccolo's heart raced and blood pounded in his ears. He listened for any sounds nearby but there was nothing.

Arthur opened the stairwell door and moved into the enclosed area. There was someone speaking on one of the floors below in a low voice, though with the echo Niccolo couldn't tell what he was saying. He made out the word 'priest', though.

Arthur leaned over the railing with his gun, waited a second, and then fired off two quick darts in rapid succession. Niccolo heard the twang of the compressed air releasing and then something heavy thudded to the floor, a body. A second later, another body thudded onto the hard floor next to it.

This was followed by a lot of shouting from below, though it was muffled and coming from out in the lobby of the hotel. Someone screamed and then something heavy crashed to the floor.

"Come on," Arthur said, rushing forward down the stairs and fishing more darts out of his pocket. He deftly loaded the new ones into the gun and chambered one.

They reached the lobby level of the stairwell and Niccolo ran through. Arthur grabbed his arm and jerked him back out of the way. Not a second too soon, either: the sudden barking of gunshots from outside the stairwell and Niccolo heard it pounding into the wood around him.

"Not that way," Arthur admonished. "Down."

"What?"

Arthur pointed further down the stairs leading to the basement and then shoved Niccolo that direction. Niccolo moved quickly, though his legs felt like rubber. He glanced over his shoulder and expecting at any moment for an enemy to appear in the doorway with a rifle and shoot them in the back.

They reached the bottom of the staircase. The

basement door was locked, but it was shoddy and weak. Arthur kicked it open on his second try; it made a loud sound as it crashed open. This door led into a dirty and dingy staff laundry room that smelled of must and mildew.

They ran inside just as he heard shouting from the lobby up above. Arthur passed Niccolo and headed deeper into the room, ignoring the motion. A man appeared over the railing, holding a shotgun, but Niccolo and Arthur were out of sight before he fired.

Arthur weaved around the laundry carts and past the running washers and dryers of the basement laundry room, pausing at the windows on their left as he went. Niccolo struggled just to keep up: his knees were stiff; the adrenaline felt like it would make his heart explode in his chest.

Finally, Arthur stopped and pointed at one of the windows. "That one. Open it."

He didn't wait for Niccolo to respond, instead walking back past him in the direction they had come. Niccolo heard footsteps scuffing across the pavement floor as Arthur raised his gun.

He fired off two quick shots and Niccolo heard a groan. Arthur slid more darts out of his pocket and loaded them into the chamber.

The window in question was just above their headline and small. It was a tight fit to squeeze through, and worse it was a permanent fixture and didn't actually have a hinge to open it. Niccolo felt around the edges and wouldn't be easy to pry out, either.

"Hurry up," Arthur said.

"I am!"

More gunshots echoed in the laundry room,

causing Niccolo to tense up, and then Arthur fired the dart gun again. It sounded weak compared to the pistols that were being fired at them. "We don't have a lot of time."

Niccolo panicked and fought the fear back down. He rushed over to a loose brick on the wall, and with a little bit of effort pried it loose.

Busting the window would leave shards, so he hurried over to one of the nearby laundry carts as well. He yanked out a loose sheet and wrapped it around his fist. He heard more gunshots but focused only on his task.

"Alright," he said to himself, hefting the brick. "Here goes nothing."

He tossed the brick as hard as he could at the glass. It shattered the window with ease and sailed right through, scattering shards everywhere. He gritted his teeth in satisfaction and rushed over to it.

There were still huge shards attached to the empty sill and he didn't have anything left to bust them out of the way.

"Oops."

"Anytime now," Arthur shouted, ducking behind a machine as one of their pursuers opened fire. He popped over the top, launched another dart. Another man fell to the ground. "Out of darts."

"Doesn't matter. Come on," Niccolo said.

He bunched up the sheet around his knuckles, knocked the remaining glass out of the way with his fist, and then laid the cloth down across the bottom sill to climb over.

He grabbed onto the sides of the window, let out a deep breath, and then wriggled his way through. It was a tight squeeze, but he slipped out after only a few seconds. He was careful not to cut himself on any of the glass shards on the mulch outside, and then once he was clear he brushed himself off and ducked behind some bushes.

Arthur came out a few seconds later, moving with considerably more grace than Niccolo had. He nodded toward the sheet.

"Smart thinking."

"What now?"

Arthur pointed and Niccolo saw that their car was parked only a few dozen feet away.

"That's why you picked that window?" Niccolo said.

"Yep. Come on."

They rushed over and climbed into the car, and a second later they were moving. Niccolo heard more gunshots behind them from the basement window, along with shouted curses.

They were out of range for any of the shots to land. Arthur went over a short curb in front of them. They bounced and jostled across their on their way over.

And then they were on the paved road heading away from the hotel. Niccolo's blood kept pumping, but the adrenaline was wearing off and he was exhausted. It was a weighty exhaustion that made it hard to keep his eyes open.

"Who were they?"

"Local cultists," Arthur said. "I'd bet anything on it."

"How did they know we are here? Where are we going?"

"No clue for your first question. The library for the second. We need to get to Desiree in case they know about her, too."

A chilling thought. Niccolo sucked in air and willed the black dots in his vision to go away.

They drove back into the city and toward library where she was doing research.

Everything was quiet, but it was ominous in his heightened state of awareness: a car parked just around the corner of the library felt like another threat, and Niccolo found himself completely on edge.

"Wait here," Arthur said, parking just in front of the library. "I'll be right back. Don't do anything stupid."

Niccolo nodded, too tired to object. Arthur disappeared into the library and he sunk lower into his seat, hiding his face. Niccolo scanned the area surrounding the car. He kept looking for any signs of a nearby threat, half expecting a car to roll up next to them at any moment.

Arthur reappeared only a few seconds later, Desiree in tow. They moved quickly across the parking lot, her with a stack of printouts in hand. She was confused and a little scared as she climbed into the backseat.

"What's going on? What happened?"

"We were attacked," Niccolo answered. "Someone came to the hotel and tried to kill us."

They headed back out onto the road.

"Holy crap. So we can't go back?"

"No," Arthur said. "Now we have to keep moving. Find somewhere else to lay low until I can figure out how they knew we were there."

"And then what?" Desiree asked. "What do we do next?"

"No clue," Arthur replied. "I'll call Frieda and get us a safe house to stay at. I didn't know there was a cult cell in the city, so I'll see if there were any records of them."

"A cell?"

"A group of cultists. The Ninth Circle operates in independent cells, each unaware of and separated from the others. Makes it impossible to strike at more than one cell at a time."

"No central leadership," she said. "Smart."

"Yeah, but in general we know where they are operating, even if we don't know the cell itself. I didn't know there was one in Ohio. It must be new. I counted six at the hotel, probably more, so they could be a fairly sizable group, too."

"Six?" she asked. "How did you guys escape?"

"A lot of luck. They were heavily armed, but Niccolo saw them coming. We were able to get out of there before they could trap us in our room. I doubt we'll get so lucky a second time, though."

"Do you think they are working with Jeremy?"

"I don't know," Arthur replied. "But my guess is that they are."

"Maybe the girl," Niccolo said, turning to face forward again.

"What do you mean?"

"We don't know what she's capable of. Maybe she told them where to look.'

Arthur shrugged. "Maybe."

"You would think it would get easier," Niccolo muttered, shaking his head.

"What would get easier?"

"Getting shot at. You would think I would start to get used to it. How many times have I been shot at now? Four?"

Arthur laughed. "You never get used to it. Getting

shot at will never stop being a terrible experience."

"I think I know where we need to go," Desiree interrupted suddenly, unfolding her stack of papers. "It's a longshot, but Leopold served as a chaplain at a nearby hospital and his service there was why he eventually got removed from his post at Saint Thomas Church and kicked out of Athens. That's what I was researching before you guys showed up."

"What do you mean?"

"The hospital reported his treatment of women and children to the authorities. People were angry and it turned public support against him."

"Makes sense," Niccolo said. "Whatever he did at a church could be overlooked or hidden by the Vatican, but a hospital services multiple communities. It would be much more difficult to keep the truth away from public attention there. It would explain why they finally relocated him."

"That's the way it looks."

"First we need to learn more about the cult," Arthur said. "I need to find out why they were after us to begin with."

"You said yourself that they were working with Jeremy."

"Yeah, but how did Jeremy know where to send them?" Arthur asked. He shook his head. "I don't like this. Something is wrong."

"Maybe," Desiree said, "But we don't have a lot of time or other options. I think we should get to the Hospital, because my guess is that's where Jeremy is planning to go next."

"I agree with Desiree," Niccolo said. "It's the best lead we've got."

"Alright," Arthur replied with a shrug. "Then let's

go check it out."

Chapter 11

Megyn's mood annoyed Jeremy. Ever since they had first gone to Saint Thomas church she started to withdraw, and each hour that passed it only got worse. Now, after their trip to the junkyard, she would barely talk to him. She would barely even look at him, in fact.

Worse, they still hadn't found a safe place to hide out after the priest and his pet hunter had invaded their sanctuary. Jeremy had considered asking the cultists for sanctuary, but when he had seen their disgusting living conditions and the way in which they looked at him and Megyn he had elected not to. Instead, they were still living in their car and being driven around by his demonic chauffeur.

Nothing was going quite as planned. It was taking a lot longer to put things into motion and turning out to be much more difficult than Jeremy had originally anticipated. If only their Father could have lived, they would be able to get through this without any problem and finish enacting their agenda against these people.

"How much longer until the ingredients are prepared?" he asked.

He saw the driver's eyes in the rearview mirror. "An hour. Maybe less. Once the organs have dried out they will be ready for the ritual."

Jeremy nodded. He had helped Leopold with the summoning ritual multiple times back in Everett, but he didn't know every step in the preparation of the other ingredients.

Leopold had dried out the organs and then burned them to ash before using them in the ritual. He didn't have any good way to dry them, so he just set them outside on the road.

They weren't drying as much as he hoped, though. It was too cold outside, but he had to consider himself lucky they weren't freezing solid either.

The demon knew enough about the ritual to fill in the missing steps, but he told Jeremy this was an important one. Important or not, Jeremy was just about done with it. He would start burning them to ashes soon one way or another.

Then, they would be underway in summoning their army, and with it they would be able to wreak havoc on the town. He had chosen their initial target already as well, a viable and barely protected target with a lot of potential vessels in it.

Things were finally moving in their favor and it wouldn't be long until they had earned vengeance for their father against this petty little town.

So, why was Megyn still so depressed?

"Lighten up," he said, swatting her arm and smiling at her. "We're about to accomplish everything our father set out for us. We're about to win."

She winced away from him, drawn out of her reverie. "I didn't realize..."

His smile evaporated. "Didn't realize what?"

She hesitated. "That you...that we would have to kill so many people."

"What did you think was going to happen? What did you honestly expect our plan to be? Were we just going to adopt kittens and puppies or something? Our Father taught you how to suffocate people until they are dead, and you knew he wasn't showing you this so you could dance with unicorns. You knew what the plan would be."

"This is different..."

"Different than what?"

"Than what he said—"

"It isn't," he insisted. "You just want it to be different because you are scared. This is exactly what we trained for all of these last years. This is what we prepared our minds to do, and now we are finishing it. You didn't think we would kill people? Well this is war. People die. If not them, then it would be us."

"Would it?"

"Of course it would. We are different, Megyn. You know what society does to those who are different."

Megyn didn't look convinced by his argument, which only annoyed Jeremy more. He could hardly believe that after all of the years preparing she still didn't want to go through with this.

She never would have challenged Leopold like this.

He scoffed at her and waved his hand in dismissal. "I don't get you. I don't understand how you can claim to believe in our Father's cause, but when push comes to shove you aren't willing to follow through. I can't believe you are so weak."

"This wasn't what our Father wanted," she whispered. "He wanted to show the world who we are. Not just what we can do."

"This is exactly what he wanted. He wanted revenge against the people that hurt him. He wanted to punish the heretics that stood against him, and he wanted to wake the world up to the fact that we exist and that we are powerful. All he ever wanted was a better future for us, and that means we have to take it by force."

That had been something Leopold told him hundreds of times: the Bishop's only goal was to make life better for his adopted children, no matter the cost. He gathered them together and taught them how to use their abilities.

In fact, his original plan when he first started this crusade had been to gather the children up and bring them to the Vatican to force the leaders of the church to open their eyes about the special gifts children like Jeremy and Megyn had. He intended to barter a better life for the children and a higher station for himself: the children would have been his ticket to becoming a Cardinal.

The loftier ambitions of garnering international attention hadn't materialized until much later when Jeremy came into the picture. Jeremy had been the child that changed everything, and that was when he began working with the cult.

It had started as an information gathering alliance between him and The Ninth Circle to seek out more children across the globe, but then he discovered what Jeremy could do not only in manipulating people, but in helping lesser demons control their vessels they might otherwise be too weak to dominate.

Normally, Jeremy knew, it took an extensive amount of time and patience for a demon to take control of a host. Weeks, sometimes months of work, and even then it was never a guaranteed thing. The host and parasite would battle for dominance, and more often than not the host would win out. Not many demonic entities were strong enough to seize control on their own.

With Jeremy, though, everything changed. He could cow the human host into submission and help the demon to gain control, and when that control waned he could beat the human back to ensure the demon maintained control. He took a monumental task and trivialized it.

When Bishop Glasser discovered what he was capable of, his ambitions had skyrocketed and he developed a new plan, this time to wake the world up and achieve even greater glory. Not simply the Vatican and not for a seat at the table. He wanted something more.

The only problem was, Jeremy wasn't sure what that something was.

Leopold had shown Jeremy minor pieces of plan and how to execute them, but he'd never told him what the endgame was. Punishment and revenge were byproducts, yes, but when Megyn attacked the church and hospital, he and Leopold were supposed to be well out of the country, either in Europe or India laying low.

And, none of that was supposed to happen until after they gathered that last stupid child in India.

The Bishop had turned away from Jeremy in the final months. His eyes were set on a younger boy who he claimed was the one. Haatim, a young Indian child, was the only person Leopold had talked about in those final days.

He had become the Bishop's favorite, even though they had never met in person. Leopold had wasted months getting his family to come to Everett, hiding out in his manor and casting out his net. He had put all his plans on hold for him.

Perhaps the cult leader had been correct back at the salvage yard: maybe Leopold *had* changed his mind about the final attack; maybe he was abandoning his grand ambitions and he was planning something new using Haatim.

They would never know, and just thinking about it made Jeremy furious. If their father had changed the plan, then Jeremy should have been told about it. He should have been the one the Bishop trusted. Not some silly cultists in Ohio and not some little boy from India. They didn't need that stupid Indian child, had never needed him. They didn't need anything except the family they already had: they had their army, their plan, and the time to do what needed to be done.

Because of Leopold they had failed.

It was the first time Jeremy had admitted it to himself. Those words that encompassed the idea that the Bishop was the weak point of their family. Jeremy accepted it now. Just thinking about it made Jeremy feel sick, but he embraced it nonetheless.

The Bishop had been weak and a fool.

Jeremy wouldn't follow in the footsteps of a weak man. He knew it subconsciously, but now he was aware consciously as well. Of course this wasn't the Bishop's plan, to kill these people and summon the army ... Jeremy had just been lying to himself. This was his plan.

He would succeed where the arrogant old fool had failed.

"We will finish what our Father started," he muttered. His voice slowly rose in volume and intensity. "We will finish the war and achieve even more than Leopold ever dreamed possible. He wanted us to be better than him, and we are."

"We don't need to do this—"

"People will die, Megyn," Jeremy said, grabbing her chin and forcing her to meet his eyes. "What I need to know right now is whether or not you will be one of them. So, are you with me, or are you against me?"

Megyn slid across the seat farther away from him, but he refused to let go. He held her chin, squeezing until he knew it was painful. "Jeremy, you're hurting me…"

"I need to know if you will see this through. Tonight we will finish executing the Bishop's plan for Ohio, and we will punish everyone who ever did him harm. They will try to stop us, so I need to know right now if you are going to help me or stand in my way. I need to know, Megyn, because I can't stand around worrying about whether you have the stomach to honor our father."

Megyn's shaking hand slowly crept up to the door handle. Her chin quivered. "Jeremy … you're scaring me."

"Tell me right now, Megyn. Will you be at my side… or not?"

A long while passed. Finally, Megyn let out a sigh and lowered her hand from the door. He saw the submission in her eyes and he had won. Jeremy released his grip on her chin and there was a painful red mark where his hand had been.

"Of course I will help you, Jeremy. I want this as much as you do…I just…"

He nodded. She slumped low in the seat. He had used the stick, now it was time for the carrot.

He took a deep breath. "I know what you mean, Megyn. I'm sorry to scare you. I know what you are dealing with, and I'm dealing with it too. It's harder than we thought," he lied. "But together we can do this. Once we finish at the Hospital we can move on and gather some of the other children. Our vengeance will be taken care of and we will be able to go on with our lives."

"You promise?"

"I promise."

She leaned across the car seat and gave him a hug.

"Thank you."

He hugged her back, patting her gently. "Always, little sister."

"Is the ash ready? It's been burning for over an hour."

"Yes," the demon said. "It is ready. A small amount will be required for each demon we wish to summon, along with the other offerings."

"Good. Then let's get moving," he said.

Megyn was fast asleep on the backseat of the car. She was exhausted and hadn't been sleeping well, but that was to be expected. It would be a busy night, after all.

He still didn't fully trust her, but right now he didn't much care. Once he had his army summoned and ready to do his bidding, she would no longer matter.

He climbed into the front seat of the car next to the driver, holding the Tupperware container of ashes that the demon had prepared for him. It was mixed with the other ingredients to perform the summoning ritual, and each little scoop would bring one demon. They represented his future and everything that he knew he could achieve.

"Let's go," he said. "Time to finish this."

Chapter 12

Frieda glanced over at the passenger seat of her little rental car at the little girl sitting next to her. She was second-guessing her decision to bring Abigail along on this early morning raid to grab Curtis.

Today they were finally going to collect the Vatican child. Mikael had called her the previous evening to tell them where to meet. Curtis had never actually hurt anyone, so she didn't have to worry about dragging Abigail into danger.

Mikael wouldn't be happy about her decision to bring Abi, which to be honest Frieda considered another bonus of having the little girl along. She was getting tired of dealing with Mikael and would be happy once she was finally rid of the arrogant priest.

"Remember when we get there that you have to stay in the car."

"I know," Abigail said, yawning. "I just stay in the car while you guys go inside."

"And don't leave the car."

"Okay."

"Abi, promise me you won't leave the car."

Abigail frowned at her. "I promise."

Frieda worried that she was allowing Abigail to be a little too involved in her life as a hunter, but she felt it was important that Abigail understood what they were doing.

Of course, even staying in the car, Abigail could barely stop fidgeting. She drummed her fingers on the car door. She hadn't even been difficult to wake up this morning around two o'clock. She was too excited that they were finally going to finish this job and be able to move on from their smelly hotel room. She had even been ready this morning before Frieda.

They were going after Curtis in his home. Mikael had trailed him back to his residence and determined that the best time to grab him would be in the early morning before anyone in the neighborhood was awake.

He was living in a rundown section of the city in a rent-controlled apartment that was registered under a false identity the Bishop had created. Most of the surrounding apartments were empty and unoccupied, unable to pass local inspections, and even if things went sideways they were still not likely to have any police interference.

When they pulled up to the meeting place she saw Mikael. He had ditched his usual garb for loose fitting black trousers and a navy-blue t-shirt. He walked up to her car as she parked in the alley, and then frowned when she saw that Abigail was inside with her.

"What is she doing here?"

"I don't exactly have a babysitter."

"Don't worry, I'm just going to stay in the car," Abigail said.

"She'll be fine outside," Frieda said.

"If you say so."

"Are we ready?"

"Yes. Curtis is inside sleeping. This should be easy to grab and it shouldn't take more than a couple of minutes."

"Alright," Frieda said. "Then, let's do this."

***

Abigail tapped her fingers against the doorframe and made little popping noises with her teeth.

She pounded her hand against the armrest and let out a deep sigh.

"I am so bored!" she said to no one in particular.

She had promised Frieda that she would wait in the car, but she hadn't really thought she would get left behind for this long. It had already been at least twenty minutes. Abigail had tried falling back asleep, but she was too excited.

Frieda and the church guy had left about ten minutes ago, heading toward an entrance around the front of the building. She didn't know how long they would be gone, but she hoped they were almost done.

These last days had been spent just sitting in a hotel room and waiting. She had thought that being on a mission would be better than the normal time she spent with Frieda, since most of the time she just rode around in a car while they met with Hunters. They didn't get to do anything or move around, just sit in a hotel room and wait for something to happen.

Frieda had told her she should take a nap while she was waiting, but she couldn't sleep. Even if she didn't get to come along when they actually went into the apartment and grabbed up Curtis, it was still a pleasant change to be included in—

Abigail suddenly spotted movement on the third floor of the building; one of the windows above the fire escape was opening.

She unbuckled herself and leaned forward, peering up at it. It was a dark night and there weren't a lot of lights on in the city, so she didn't know if maybe her eyes were just playing tricks on her.

The window shifted in its slot again before sliding

up. A second later something came flying out the window, landing on the grated railway of the fire escape. It looked like a bag.

A moment later and a leg followed it out, followed by the rest of a body, and then the person stood up on the railing. He was scanning the area, frantic and jittery on the fire escape.

It was Curtis.

He picked up his bag and then ran along the fire escape toward the stairs leading down. He rushed down that first set to a lower level, and then rushed around to the drop ladder that went into the alley where Frieda's car was parked.

Just as he reached the drop ladder, Frieda came scrambling out the window on the third floor. She rolled onto the railing, and leaned over the railing.

"He's running!" she shouted back over her shoulder.

Then she rushed over to the stairwell leading down, giving chase. Curtis dropped from the ladder about five feet to land awkwardly on the ground.

Mikael was only now climbing out of the window behind Frieda.

Abigail hesitated for only a second before opening the car door. Curtis was a lot bigger than she was, but she could at least slow him down.

He was just reaching the ground when Abigail got out of the car, and he came running toward her.

"Hey, you!" she shouted, moving to intercept him.

Curtis tried to dodge her, but she caught the hem of his sweatshirt. He tried to shake her loose, but she kept a grip and got dragged along.

He stopped, grabbing her wrist to yank her free.

Only...

That didn't happen.

Everything stopped instead, and it was as though time itself froze. Abigail and Curtis locked eyes, and she felt a rush of terror from him.

As soon as he touched her skin, she felt something course down her arm. Instinctively, she let go of his sweater, but he didn't let go of her wrist. His eyes were wild, like a mad dog, and his lips started quivering.

There was an intense and overwhelming feeling of hopelessness in the pit of Abigail's stomach, and she almost fell to the ground. It was like a wave crashed over her, and all of the energy poured out of her body like a river. She closed her eyes and gritted her teeth, letting it pass over her.

Gradually, it subsided.

She heard a sobbing sound from the ground in front of her, and it took a second to realize Curtis was no longer touching her wrist. Suddenly, someone touched her shoulder. Frieda had a concerned expression on her face, but she wasn't directing it at Abigail.

She was looking at the lump in front of Abigail. Curtis was lying there, curled into the fetal position and sobbing. His eyes were clenched closed and he was shaking and muttering to himself.

"What...what happened?" Abigail asked, bewildered.

She heard pounding footsteps and suddenly Mikael was standing there. He grabbed Abigail roughly, shaking her, and he had an angry look in his eyes.

"What did you do?"

"Let go of her," Frieda said, stepping closer.

"You're hurting me," Abigail cried out. Mikael

squeezed her arms very tightly and she winced in pain. "Let go of me!"

"What did you do to him?"

"Stop this at once!" Frieda ordered. "I won't warn you again."

Mikael ignored her. "Tell me! What did you do to Curtis? Why is he like that?"

Frieda snatched Mikael by the wrist and jerked him toward her. Mikael released Abigail's arms and aimed an open-hand slap at Frieda's face.

His blow never even came close.

Frieda stepped closer to him, blocking his strike with her arm, and then she punched him twice in the chest, knocking him back. She jabbed her fist into his throat, collapsing his air pipe. He stumbled back, clutching at his throat to draw a breath. Frieda stepped in closer.

She spun and swept her leg, tripping him to the ground, and then put her boot on his throat.

"I said I wouldn't ask you again."

Mikael struggled, and Frieda dug her heel.

"You're not going to touch her, are you?"

He shook his head and tapped at the boot, struggling for air. Frieda held her foot there for an extra second and then pulled it away.

Mikael laid on the ground for a moment, sucking in air, and then climbed shakily to his feet. He stumbled a little bit, red faced and wary, and rubbed at his throat.

"What did she do to him?" he asked, quieter this time. "Why is he on the ground like this? What happened?"

"Nothing."

"Don't lie to me, Frieda. What is she?"

"She's only a girl. She didn't do anything," Frieda replied, standing protectively in front of Abigail. "You have your target. Gather Curtis up. Go."

"Tell me what she is, and I will go. I must report this to the Vatican."

"No. I already told you. She is just a girl."

"I need to take her—"

"I told you to go," Frieda said, her voice taking on a tone Abigail had never heard before. A chill shot down her young spine and she took a half step back from Frieda. "Don't make me say it again."

Mikael hesitated for a second longer, then he picked Curtis up. Curtis was still crying and completely out of his mind as he was slung unceremoniously over Mikael's shoulder.

"The church will hear of this."

Mikael walked away. He headed out of the alleyway, glanced back one last time, and then disappeared around the corner.

"Get in," Frieda said.

They climbed quickly into the car and she tore off down the road, heading away from the apartment complex toward the freeway.

She drove quickly, as though running from something, and she didn't speak at all. Abigail thought to say something, but she was hesitant now. Frieda had sounded furious, but more than that she was scary.

Abigail had never thought of Frieda as dangerous before. She was always so calm and laid back. This was a side of her she'd never seen before.

She didn't like it.

They headed for the interstate and going northeast. They kept traveling in silence, and gradually the weight of the silence built up until Abigail couldn't take it anymore.

Finally, Abigail said, "I...I'm sorry. I didn't mean to do that—"

"You did nothing wrong," Frieda interrupted, staring straight ahead.

"Are you mad at me?"

"No, of course not. Why would I be mad?"

Abigail frowned, staring out the window. They drove in silence for another few minutes before Abigail fell asleep. Frieda didn't say anything else, and Abigail was too afraid to speak again. She knew she'd messed up, she just didn't know how to make it right.

Frieda woke her up later at a fast food restaurant. The sun out now and Frieda looked exhausted. She still spoke very little to Abigail, and wouldn't make eye contact.

"We left our stuff."

"I already sent a friend back to retrieve it. I didn't want to be there in case..."

She didn't finish the statement. Abigail waited for her to continue, but Frieda just returned to her meal and looked away.

"In case what? Do you think Mikael was going to tell on me?"

"No," Frieda said. "I think he was going to tell on me."

"What do you mean?"

Frieda hesitated. "Nothing. Never mind. Finish your breakfast. We need to get back on the road and head to Ohio."

"To see Arthur?"

"Yeah," she said. "To see Arthur."

Frieda sat like the weight of the entire world was on her shoulders, and she was lost in her thoughts.

Abigail watched her for a moment and then realized that she had been wrong: Frieda wasn't angry.
She was scared.

Chapter 13

Debra Walker sat in the waiting room of the hospital emergency room with a wrinkled and worn magazine opened on her lap. Her foot was tapping impatiently on the hard linoleum floor and her hands kept clenching.

She was staring at an article about a new beauty mask that would revolutionize her life but none of the words were sinking in. She'd been reading the same advertisement for the last half hour.

Her eyes kept wandering over to the emergency room double doors where they had wheeled her husband through a short while ago. He had complained of chest pain while they were back at home eating dinner, collapsed onto the floor, and now they were here. Debra had never been as scared in her entire life as those ten minutes spent waiting for an ambulance to arrive.

The nurse said that Frank had already been taken to some other department of the hospital to get a chest scan, which was why they kept her out in the waiting room instead of the emergency area. He still had to get one test or another to figure out what the actual problem was so they could fix it.

Probably another heart attack, she knew, and if it was then it would be his second one in the last three years. The first hadn't been much at all, just an ache and new daily medicine he had to take, but this time it was different. This time...

It wasn't good, that's all she knew. He hadn't been taking the medicine like he was supposed to and she kept telling him that he needed to be more consistent. He was stubborn and forgetful, and now they were both paying the price. She understood that this time he might not make it through to the other side.

The nurse was supposed to come get her and bring her back to his emergency room once Frank's tests were over with, but so far no one had come out to speak with her. It was past nine at night and the entire hospital was quiet. She didn't know if that was normal, but it was a sleepy little town and she assumed the lack of patients was because it was so cold outside.

Still, if they weren't busy, why was it taking so long?

The more time passed by the more certain she became that something was really wrong with her husband. It was a creeping fear in the back of her mind. That was why no one had come out to see her, the little voice of fear told her. No one wanted to be the one to deliver the bad news that she wouldn't see her husband again.

Her fingers clutched at the magazine and she could feel them shivering. It was cold in the waiting room, but not that cold. She forced herself to relax and set the magazine on the table next to her.

Maybe they were just slow in getting the results back. Or maybe they had forgotten to come and tell her what they had found. No news was good news, right? That's what they always said. Maybe everything was fine and she was just being paranoid.

Debra hadn't called her son or her daughters yet. They would rush over as soon as she told them, of course, but the thought of making those calls paralyzed her with fear. As soon as she told them what had happened it would all become real.

She knew she needed to call them, though.

There was a sudden crashing sound from the other side of the door to the emergency room, and Debra jumped a little in her seat. It sounded like a bunch of metal pans had dumped to the floor and bounced around.

She dropped the magazine, heart racing, and stood up from her seat. There were no other sounds. Slowly, she made her way over to the entry doors to the emergency bay to look through the square little windows in the center of each door.

The entire emergency department appeared empty: even this late at night while they weren't busy she should have seen employees and doctors moving around, right?

Debra was suddenly aware of how alone she was in the waiting room, and how disturbing the hospital felt without any activity. The receptionist had said she would be right back, hadn't she?

How long ago was that?

Must have been at least thirty minutes.

Debra blinked as though suddenly coming awake from a dream. She had been so absorbed in her prayers and worries about Frank she'd completely lost track of time. Had it really been that long since anyone was out here?

She hadn't even noticed the receptionist leave, too wrapped up in her own thoughts. It wasn't normal for them to leave that post for more than a couple of minutes at a time to use the bathroom, was it?

The lights flickered.

She glanced up just as the antiseptic overhead lights steadied back to a normal glow, frowning. Sit down and relax, part of her brain told her, but another voice warned her that something was very wrong. The place shouldn't be this empty or quiet, and what were the odds of a hospital losing power long enough to cause the lights to flicker?

After a short internal debate, that second voice won out. Something was wrong, and that meant Frank might not be getting the help he needed. She needed to check it out and make sure her husband was okay.

She set her hand against the cold double bay doors that led back into the emergency department and took a steadying breath. There wasn't a lock, but there was a sign warning that only authorized personnel were allowed through.

She hesitated for another few seconds, listening at the doorway for any sounds of movement. She had to check it out to make sure that everything was okay with her husband and that he was getting the help he needed. Never mind that every fiber in her being was screaming for her to turn and run away.

Right?

Slowly, Debra pushed the double doors open. Somewhere further in the emergency department a machine was steadily beeping. She heard a rasping breathing sound from ahead and to the right, but nothing else. No footsteps, no people talking, nothing. The hair stood up on the back of her neck.

She tiptoed down the hallway, footsteps echoing around her, and turned the first corner. The first thing she saw down this hallway was a middle-aged man lying on the floor about ten feet ahead of her, covered in blood. She took a sharp step back, covering her mouth with her hand. He was still alive with what looked to be a deep knife wound on the side of his neck.

More blood was also spilling from his chest, and it seemed like he might have been stabbed. The man groaned, and when he saw her he stuck a bloody hand out toward her, desperately trying to reach her. There was a terrified look in his eyes that cut to her very core, a primal fear at his inability to draw breath as his blood was pumped out of his body.

No one was helping him. Someone should have been helping him, right? Where was the staff? Where were the doctors and nurses? What had happened back here to cause this man to start bleeding?

It felt like she had stepped into The Twilight Zone, but this was real. It should have been a dream, but she knew in her heart that it wasn't. This was happening; this man was really dying.

It looked as though the dying man had stumbled out of one of the nearby curtained rooms and fallen onto a cart of bedpans. He had finally collapsed to the floor, leaving a trail of blood along the way. Scattered metal pans lay all around him, many covered in his pooling blood.

Run, part of her said.

Help him, the other objected.

She felt a tear slip down her cheek as confused emotions ripped around in her body. Her chest ached and she felt her body lock up: helplessness, fear, confusion, and more paralyzed her in place.

Seconds ticked past.

"Hello?" she called out, taking a tentative step down the hallway toward the dying man. Her voice echoed back to her. "Is anyone there?"

The department split from here further off to her right down another hallway, and there were more curtained bays along both sides. It was a fifteen bed emergency department. Right now all of the curtains were pulled closed and silent.

"Hello?" she called out again, her voice echoing uncomfortably back to her. "Anybody, please!"

No answer.

She made it over to the dying man and knelt in front of him. He stared at her, eyes begging her to help him.

"Pressure," she muttered. "Put pressure on his neck."

She found a white towel, bunched it up, and pressed it down on the man's neck. He struggled, and she pushed his hands away, replacing them with the towel.

Another tear slipped down her cheek. He made gasping noises, barely conscious, and she forced the cloth down harder. Even with it soaking up the blood, however, some of it seeped through and got onto her hands.

She let out a sob, doing her best to ignore the thick red liquid as it coated her fingers and rings. It smelled horribly and she felt her stomach twisting in discomfort. This has to be a dream, she told herself, trying to convince her mind it was true. She had fallen asleep back in the lobby and this was her imagination dealing with Frank's heart attack. It couldn't be real.

She had experienced people dying in her life — both parents, a sibling, and too many more to count — but never like this. This was visceral and horrible, inescapable in a way that none of the others had been. The man on the floor was terrified as his life ebbed away, and he kept trying to talk to her even as she held the towel against his neck.

"Shh," she sobbed gently, rubbing his forehead with her free hand. Her fingers left trails of blood across his skin. "Don't speak."

He gasped and blinked, unable to focus his eyes.

"Help! Someone please help!"

The man kept gurgling and gasping, doing his best to form words. He met her eyes and grabbed her hand, leaning up.

"Stay with me. Just stay with me," she gasped. "Someone will be here soon."

The pressure wasn't working, and she could feel him dying underneath her.

What the hell was going on? This was a hospital, but no staff members were in the emergency room to save this man's life? Her husband was somewhere deeper in this building and something was terribly wrong.

If this was happening here, what must be happening to him?

The dying man's eyes slipped closed and he took another rasping breath. Debra couldn't believe that this was happening and knew she wasn't going to be able to save him. The hospital lights flickered around her and she let out a sob.

"Please. Please, stay with me."

The grip on her hand loosened as his life ebbed away. He was about to die, she realized, and more tears streamed down her cheeks.

"Someone please!" she screamed at the empty emergency room around her. "This man needs help! Please! I don't know what to do!"

His eyes suddenly shot open, and his grip on her hand tightened almost enough to hurt. She jerked back, but he didn't let go.

He leaned his head up the tiniest bit from the floor, looked her squarely in the eyes, and mumbled something to her.

Then, his eyes slipped closed and his head fell back to the floor. The blood stopped pumping out of his neck.

She knelt there for what felt like forever in shock and confusion. He was no longer dying, she knew: he was dead.

That wasn't all, though. He had spoken to her, and the word floated in her thoughts just out of reach, difficult to focus on. It took her a second to realize what it was the man had whispered to her with his final breath.

Run.

She never got the chance.

"We can actually still use him," a voice said behind her cut in suddenly.

Debra let out a little scream and stumbled to the side, sliding her knee into the man's blood and almost falling. Her dress and arms were covered in his blood and felt sticky on her skin.

The voice sounded like it had come from a kid. Debra climbed to her feet and spun, letting go of the blood-soaked towel and backing further down the emergency room hallway.

A teenage boy stood there behind her, blocking her path. He had brown hair and dirt-stained clothes on. Mud caked his clothing and his shoelaces were frayed and worn.

"Even if he dies," the boy said nonchalantly, "he can still serve as a vessel. There will be limitations, of course, as it isn't ideal to use a corpse. Still, he can be of use to us. It was unfortunate for me that he tried to run ... but, without that, I never would have found you."

His eyes were flat and empty, completely and utterly devoid of emotion. He stared at Debra, studied her, and she felt a chill creep down her spine. Something about the dismissive way he viewed her made her feel cold.

"Who ... who are you?"

"Pardon me, where are my manners? My name is Jeremy Caldwell. Who are you?"

She took a hesitant step backwards. "Debra," she said, barely managing to get the word out. "Where ... where is everyone else? Where are the doctors and nurses?"

"Here and there," he offered, waving his hand. "Some of them made fine vessels. Others ... not so much, but that was to be expected. This one thought he could escape and nearly made it to the exit. Can you imagine what would have happened if he made it outside?"

"What is going on?"

Jeremy stepped closer. "There weren't actually as many people in the hospital as I expected or would have liked. I planned to come later in the day so there wouldn't be too many people to contend with, but I think I might have misjudged and arrived too late in the day. It doesn't really matter, though, because having a little bit extra on hand doesn't hurt and I can always summon more."

"What?"

He smiled, another step closer. "Lucky for me, we didn't even know you were out there. I think, though, that you will work out perfectly. Definitely better than using his corpse as a vessel."

"You're scaring me? What's going on?"

"Oh, am I now? Am I scaring you?"

He took another menacing step forward.

"Stay back."

Suddenly, she felt an intense urge to collapse to her knees. She almost did, too, before she fought the urge and backed away. She felt her knees wavering as the intrusive idea of kneeling kept vying for control. Something about the suggestion felt wrong, like it wasn't her idea at all. It was foreign.

"A tough one?" he asked. "I like that. I enjoy a good challenge once in a while."

Debra felt her mind begin to get fuzzy and it became hard to focus. Something was very, very wrong and suddenly her thoughts weren't her own. She had no idea what was happening, but she knew she couldn't stay here with this creepy boy for another second.

She turned and ran down the hallway away from him. She went past the little emergency beds with their curtains pulled closed. She passed one that was only partly closed and inside she saw what looked to be a dead woman lying on the hospital bed.

Debra was running harder than she had in her last fifty years and her muscles strained under the effort.

And then suddenly she wasn't moving.

It felt as though she was were running through thick water, and then the water changed form to ice. She froze in place, and it felt as though her entire body was encased in some hard substance. She couldn't feel anything on her skin, but that didn't change the fact that she couldn't move.

Her body was still midstride, she was just no longer in control of it.

A little girl, maybe twelve years old, stepped out of one of the emergency bays in front of her. Like the boy, she as dirty and disheveled and maybe a few years his junior. If she cleaned up she would have been quite pretty with a round face and blue eyes.

She stared up at Debra, frowning, and then glanced past her to where Jeremy was standing.

Debra struggled. The grip on her was like iron, and it surrounded her completely. She couldn't do anything except strain her muscles, and the helplessness of her situation caused her to sob once more.

She heard footsteps walking up behind her, and then Jeremy stepped past. He was eyeing Debra's frozen form midstride. He stood next to the little girl.

"I'm impressed. Well done, sis."

"The cops are arriving," the little girl whispered, still staring at Debra. She looked scared and worried, almost on the verge of crying herself. "I think someone called them."

"Of course they are. I called them."

"What?"

"That was the plan. Let me know when news vans start arriving and we can get this show on the road. How are the others coming along?"

"It's taking some time for the new ones to adjust, but many are up and moving already. Only one lost control of its vessel."

"Did you...?"

She winced. "Yes. I took care of it."

"Perfect," Jeremy said, smiling up at Debra. "Lucky for us, we now have another vessel to try out. We're almost ready to start the main event, sis: time to get this show on the road!"

Chapter 14

"What on earth is happening here?" Niccolo asked, leaning across his seat to look out Arthur's window.

They drove up the road slowly toward the emergency entrance of the hospital. Arthur stopped well short of the parking lot which had been quarantined off by police vehicles. Officers were milling around and talking to one another.

There were four police cars and a swat van blocking the parking lot entrance. A television crew was also parked nearby, though the police had strung up crime scene tape to keep them at bay.

A tall blonde woman stood just outside the barricade on the far side of the parking lot with a microphone in hand. She was speaking into a camera and broadcasting the story out to doubtless many different sources. An event like this, it wouldn't be long before her coverage of the events went national.

If it hadn't already.

"Judging by the police response, some sort of attack. It looks like we've come to the right place," Arthur said.

"You think Jeremy is in there?"

Arthur drove off the road onto a grass knoll and turned the car off.

"I would bet anything on it. This is his endgame."

"What do you mean?"

"He's been collecting organs to be used in a summoning ritual, and this is where he plans to use them. The perfect place to punish the hospital that turned Leopold into an outcast."

"That makes no sense," Niccolo said, shaking his head. "None of the people inside there would have been involved in what happened to the Bishop."

"I doubt that Jeremy cares," Arthur said. "There's only one way to find out, though. Let's go."

"How are we going to get inside?" Niccolo asked. "The police have the place on a complete lockdown. You don't think they'll just let us in, do you?"

"Leave that to me."

He climbed out of the car into the cool winter air, mind working through the situation and prioritizing options. There weren't a lot of them.

"We need to deal with the reporters," Arthur said, pointing at the blonde woman. "If she manages to send out a live feed it will make this a lot harder to keep hidden."

"The truck is broadcasting," Desiree said. "See that tower on the top? That's what forms the uplink and sends the signal."

"What are you thinking?" he asked, glancing at her.

"I bet if I cut the right wires it'll shut down the uplink."

"How will you know which ones are the right ones?"

She shrugged. "When I run out of wires, I'll know I cut the right one."

He laughed. "Do you think you can get close to it?"

She nodded toward the police cars and officers. "I am guessing that right now they have other things on their minds."

"Alright then. Nothing dangerous, though. Got it?"

"Got it."

"Do you need my help?" Niccolo asked.

She shook her head. "Nah, this will be easy-peasy. I will borrow a knife if you guys have one?"

Arthur slipped a pocket knife loose and tossed it to

her. She deftly caught it.

"Don't electrocute yourself."

"I'll do my best."

She walked away from the hospital, circling around to come up behind the van and out of sight.

"Ready?"

Niccolo let out a shuddering breath and nodded.

"As I'll ever be."

They walked across the freshly cut grass toward the crime scene tape.

Arthur slid his badge free again as he headed to the barricade. He recognized one of the officers from the church a few days earlier and whistled to get his attention. The officer noticed him after a few seconds and came over to the yellow tape to talk.

"Wait here," Arthur said, heading over to speak with the officer.

The officer was overwhelmed by the entire situation. Arthur felt for him, though he was pretty sure that things would just get worse for this poor kid before the night was over.

"The FBI got called in for this?"

"Yeah."

"You don't think it's related to what happened at the church, do you?"

"We don't know anything yet, but we haven't ruled anything out," Arthur said. "What's going on here?"

"We honestly don't know. A hostage situation, though it's impossible to tell exactly what is going on inside. A kid called about fifteen minutes ago and said that someone was holding them hostage inside. He said that it was an older man and he had a gun."

"No identity of the suspect?"

"No. Right now we're being cautious and waiting

for orders. Is the FBI bringing in a hostage negotiator? Are you taking this situation over?"

"Not yet. Is your CO planning to breach?"

"Not right now. We have swat on standby and all of the entrances are covered, but so far we haven't been able to make contact by calling inside. No one in the hospital is talking."

"No one?"

He shook his head. "We called twenty different phones. No answers."

"How many hostages are inside?"

"Best estimate is around twenty people total, give or take. No one has reached out with demands yet, though, so it's all just speculation at this point."

"Thank you," Arthur said.

He nodded at the officer and then walked back over to where Niccolo was waiting.

"What's going on?" Niccolo asked. "Is it Jeremy?"

"It has to be. He said a kid called them. Twenty bucks says he called the news station, too."

"What is he doing?"

"Right now he is biding his time. This is exactly what he wants: a standoff. The longer the police wait to breach, the more people are going to see what happens. We really need for Desiree to cut that feed."

"You think he's summing more demons?"

"I think he has twenty civilians inside who are being turned as we speak."

"He will use them to attack the police."

"The police will have no choice but to use deadly force, and the entire incident will get international attention. It'll be impossible to completely cover this up."

"They can just call it a shooting or an explosion,"

Niccolo argued, shaking his head.

"Not when they see what the little girl can do. Enough people will see that to force them to ask questions. Jeremy's plan is to get enough eyeballs that we can't cover this up."

"So, what do we do?"

"I don't know," Arthur said. "We need to find a way inside and put an end to this. Do you think this place has an unlocked side door?"

Niccolo didn't answer him. He stared over Arthur's shoulder, frowning. "I think we're too late."

Arthur followed his gaze toward the emergency room entrance of the hospital and saw that the sliding door was opening. The cops exploded into motion, hiding behind their cars with guns trained on the doorway.

"Hands up!" one of the officers shouted. "Come out slowly and keep those hands in the air."

For a long while, nothing happened. The doorway stood open and waiting. Soft waiting room music spilled out into the cold night air. Occasionally one of the officers would fidget.

Nothing about this was right. He beckoned for Niccolo to follow and started walking over toward the police cars. They ducked under the yellow tape.

After about two minutes of silence a man crept into sight just inside the entrance, hands raised up above his head.

"We're unarmed," the man shouted. "Civilians!"

"Keep your hands up!" the officer shouted again. "How many are with you?"

"Fifteen!"

"Walk toward us. Slow and steady. Where is the kidnapper?"

"Still inside. He's injured."

The man started walking out of the hospital toward the police cars, hands held squarely up in the air. Behind him came a stream of other people.

Fifteen demons against ten unassuming and unprepared police.

"Crap, "Arthur said.

"Do you think...?" Niccolo started to ask. "Did Jeremy turn them?"

Arthur headed quickly over toward the barricade, scanning the group. They moved like civilians, but they were too organized. In the middle of the group, he saw, were Jeremy and a little girl.

Arthur slipped his tranquilizer gun free just as the first of the civilians made it to the line of police cars. One of the officers moved around the front of his car. He slid his gun away and patted the man down.

"Where is the man who took you all hostage? Is this everyone?"

"This is all of us," the man said. He kept his hands in the air while the cop moved from one leg to the other.

After a few seconds, the officer cleared him and moved on to the next woman in line. That first man went past the barricade and was met by a paramedic and brought to an ambulance to be checked out.

The rest of the officers kept their guns trained on the group, but Arthur could see that many of them were relaxing. Two swat team members had a quick conversation and then headed into the hospital.

Niccolo stepped up beside Arthur.

"What is Jeremy doing?"

"Spreading them out," Arthur said. "Lulling them into a false sense of security. Six cops now and two swat. They are outnumbered and don't even know they are under attack."

"We need to stop this."

"We do," Arthur said. "Ideally without getting shot. The last thing we need is to be the distraction that starts the attack."

"Then what do we do?" he whispered.

Jeremy was studying two swat team members who were huddled behind a police car and carrying heavy weapons.

Jeremy was digging his way into the mind of one of the men. Both officers were holding shotguns aimed over the back of the car and wearing full body armor. The civilians were being scattered around and directed to various ambulances, mixed into the group of first responders.

Suddenly, Jeremy smiled. He burst out laughing.

"Showtime!"

"Oh no," Arthur muttered.

Arthur raised his tranquilizer gun up. One of the officers shouted when he spotted the gun in Arthur's hand, and several other people turned to look his way.

Including the little girl.

It didn't matter though, they were all too late: Arthur squeezed the trigger.

Or, at least, he tried to.

He suddenly couldn't move his finger. Or his hand, or arm, or any other part of his body. He was just locked in place, like he was paralyzed. He fought against it, struggling to squeeze the trigger and fire the dart. He could feel his muscles straining and his hand started shaking under the pressure. He put everything he had into it. He moved his finger just enough to squeeze the trigger. He heard the twang of the dart as it fired out of the barrel of his gun, heading directly for

Jeremy's neck.

Arthur let out a hiss of satisfaction. It was over.

Only...

The dart stopped moving. About ten feet in front of Arthur's outstretched gun it simply stopped flying, hovering in midair and frozen.

Then, it dropped to the ground.

"Uh oh."

Suddenly his feet were no longer on the ground.

***

Niccolo watched Arthur go flying through the night air. He flew about four feet off the ground careening across the parking lot and slammed into a nearby car, hard, and then fell onto his side. Niccolo couldn't even tell if he was still conscious.

Or alive.

Everyone in the area stopped when Arthur went flying, frozen in place in shock. Everyone that was, except for one of the swat team members. Jeremy was staring at him, a smile on his young face. Suddenly, that armored man swung his gun to the right and pointed the barrel at the face of the swat member standing next to him.

The man pulled the trigger and the gunshot echoed across the parking lot. At that range, even with the face mask covering him, the man's head exploded into bits of brain, blood, and skull fragments. The gunshot rang echoed into the silence.

And then chaos erupted.

Jeremy's demons attacked the nearest target. Some went after police officers, screaming and snarling as they punched and kicked. Others went after civilians, scratching and clawing at their faces.

The police tried to respond to the sudden onslaught with batons and pepper spray, but there were only six officers left. The swat team member that Jeremy was controlling chambered another round, turned, and blew one of the remaining officers away.

More shooting erupted. An officer drew a baton and swung it at a civilian. His hit landed, but the woman just kept coming, snarling and vicious. She dove at the officer, clawing at his face, and he screamed in panic.

Another man bit the arm of another officer and blood ran down his chin. The officer screamed and tried to pull loose, and a chunk of arm fell to the ground.

Jeremy stood in the center of it, smiling as he surveyed the devastation. He spotted Arthur's prone form, and his smile only grew.

"Glad you could make it!" he said, walking over and kicking Arthur's shoe. Arthur didn't budge.

Seconds passed, though to Niccolo it felt like hours. He couldn't see Desiree, Arthur was down, people were screaming and shouting and punching each other.

Suddenly, a police car lifted off the ground. It flew about thirty feet through the air before smashing into an ambulance, knocking both vehicles on their sides and creating huge dents and rifts in both.

People screamed and scattered, panicking. The officers watched the car in awe, but the possessed civilians didn't even notice. They were hyper-focused only on doing as much damage to the police as they could. A man wrestled the gun free of an officer and began firing wildly.

Niccolo saw the little girl waving her hands in the

air. Her face was a mask of concentration as she turned her attention to another car. More gunshots started to bark in the area as desperate police officers finally turned their guns on the civilians.

All of it was being caught on the news crew's camera.

Niccolo slipped his tranquilizer gun out of his pocket. He only had three shots, but he realized he had to do something. The remaining darts were in the car behind them, which felt like a million miles away. He didn't know what to do or who to shoot. He didn't know how he could stop this madness.

"Her!" one of the officer's screamed, his voice ripping through the onslaught. "She's doing it! Shoot her!"

Niccolo glanced over and saw the man crouching behind his police car. Two civilians were lying on the ground around him.

This was the officer who had started shooting them instead of continuing to subdue them, he realized.

Blood was streaming down his face from a cut and his eyes were full of fear and confusion. They were also, Niccolo saw, focused squarely on the little girl standing next to Jeremy.

She was focusing on another car. It was only a few inches off of the ground. When she heard the shout and saw the officer staring at her she lost focus and the vehicle collapsed back down to the ground with a loud thud.

The officer's pistol came up.

Jeremy tried to stop him.

Niccolo raised his tranquilizer gun.

They were both too slow.

The officer pulled the trigger and his shot rang

through the night.

Chapter 15

Jeremy sized the cop mentally when he saw him aiming his gun at Megyn. He lashed out viciously, ordering him to drop the gun. It fell to the ground with a clang. Just as suddenly as Jeremy took control, though the connection was severed. The cop slumped over, a dart sticking out of his forehead. When Jeremy glanced over to where the dart had come from, he saw that the priest had been the one to shoot it.

The priest had gotten in his way for the last time. Finally, Jeremy could have his revenge. He reached out mentally, planning to seize control over the priest and force him to commit suicide. Maybe he would have him gouge out his own eyes. After all, this was the man who so heinously murdered his father, and he needed to be punished for what he had —

"Jeremy," Megyn whispered, grabbing his arm. Her grip was weak, and it broke his concentration.

He turned to her just in time to see her slump to her knees. Her mouth was open and she looked disoriented, and she was holding her hand to her shoulder, pressing it against the dirty sweater. She started to fall backward toward the ground.

"Megyn!" he cried out, reaching to catch her. She stumbled but he caught her wrist and pulled her close to him. He could feel something wet streaming down her back.

He held his hand in the light coming from the hospital behind him. Even in the dim light could see that it was blood.

"Jeremy..." she muttered, eyes blurry.

"No, no, no!" he muttered, squeezing her close to him. The bullet had gone through her shoulder and clear through, and blood was coming out both holes.

She started closing her eyes, her breath coming in shallow gasps.

"No," he said, shaking her. "Stay with me."

Suddenly something whizzed past his head. He turned and saw the priest staring at him, gun aimed at him. The dart had missed him by only inches, but if it had hit he had no doubt he would be slumped over, too.

Jeremy cursed, lashing out mentally. This time, it wasn't to control the priest, it was to hurt him. Jeremy had never really tried using his abilities just to damage before. It felt too imprecise, and he preferred just taking control.

The visceral attack, though, felt good. The priest staggered, dropping his gun and clutching his skull. He collapsed to the ground, writhing in agony, and Jeremy bared his teeth.

The satisfaction was short lived, though. Jeremy turned his attention back to Megyn and saw that she was barely conscious. She was slipping away from him.

He disliked many things about her, but the thought of losing her was as painful as anything Jeremy had ever experienced. She was the only one he had left after Leopold was taken away. If he could have taken back all of the hurtful and horrible things he'd said and thought about her over the years, he would have.

He would have given anything just to save her.

"Come on," he said, slinging her arm over his shoulder and dragging her back into the hospital. Megyn tried to walk with him, but she was more dead weight than actual help.

"Where are we going...?" she whispered.

"Inside," he said. "Stay awake, sis. Just stay with me."

He didn't miss the irony that he was carrying her back into the hospital, but everyone who could have helped her was already outside fighting.

***

It took Niccolo a long while to recover from Jeremy's mental attack. His mind was fuzzy and unfocused, similar to the after-effects of what he had experienced the first time Jeremy invaded his thoughts.

That was where the similarity ended, though. This time Jeremy hadn't controlled him, he had simply tried to hurt him. He had been successful, too, because Niccolo could barely even keep his focus long enough to stand back up. He shook his head to clear his thoughts, but it did no good. It was like the hangover from drinking at least three bottles of red wine.

He looked around, trying to get his bearings. Arthur leaned against a nearby car and was unconscious. Downed officers bled in the street while others fired at the civilians. It was mayhem, chaotic and horrific.

An overturned car burned off to his left and a police car was emitting a high-pitched whine from his right. The thrown car wrapped around a light pole, its windshield so cracked as to be opaque.

Jeremy and the little girl, though, were gone. He checked his gun and saw that he had one shot left.

Only one.

Niccolo staggered to his feet and over to where Jeremy had been standing. He saw a trail of little red droplets leading back toward the emergency room entrance of the hospital.

"Arthur," he said, collapsing to a knee and crawling

over to where his friend was lying. "Arthur, get up."

The hunter didn't budge. Niccolo shook him, but there was no effect.

He was on his own.

"Alright," he mumbled, climbing back to his feet. "Here goes nothing."

He followed the blood trail into the hospital.

***

"The signal is dead."

"You're kidding me? We lost the uplink?"

"Looks like."

"Of all the times it could lose connection, this has to be the night. At least tell me you're still recording."

"All of it. Do you want me to check if we can get it back online?"

"No. We're the only ones here. Just get the footage and we'll upload all of this tonight."

Desiree breathed a sigh of relief. Her plan had worked and the connection was severed. No signal was getting out of this parking lot.

The van was locked, so she climbed onto the roof. The dish was her target. No exposed wires, but Arthur's knife was sharp: she had simply hacked away at it until she got to the core wiring of the dish. Then, she had simply cut things until she was confident it wouldn't work anymore.

She heard gunshots and screams of pain, and the blonde reporter and her cameraman barely seemed to care. So jaded as to be disturbing as they simply stood there recording the violence and punctuating it with little reporter snippets of information.

Desiree crept away from the van and circled back around to the parking lot. People were lying on the ground, bleeding or dead. Only a few people were still fighting at all, and they looked exhausted. Broken glass and fragments of cars littered the area and the area was lit by police lights and a car fire.

It was a warzone and the smell of death was everywhere. She could smell burning gunpowder and hear the cries of the wounded. She scanned the area for Niccolo and Arthur and saw the hunter leaning up against a car near the center of the violence. She also saw what looked like Niccolo staggering into the hospital, though he was out of sight before she could verify it was him.

She crept through the parking lot to where Arthur was lying and knelt in front of him. He was unconscious and had hit his head pretty hard.

"Arthur," she said, tapping him. "Wake up."

No response. She searched around for something that would help and saw a nearby ambulance. An unconscious – or dead – man was hanging out of the back of the vehicle but it was otherwise empty.

Desiree moved over to it and gingerly stepped around the man to climb inside. She started digging around. She hadn't used the salts before but knew from a friend how –

Something touched her leg and she screamed. She jerked sideways, crashing into the ambulance equipment and falling painfully onto the cart. The man she had thought was dead was still alive.

Barely, but alive.

"Please," he muttered, crawling toward her. "Please help me."

"I will," she promised. "But right now I need to help

a friend…"

He grabbed the bottom of her shirt. "Please…I don't want to die alone…"

Desiree felt herself crying. He closed his eyes and was barely breathing. She gently extricated herself from his grip and took a step back. He was still breathing, but barely, as he slipped back into unconsciousness.

She brushed the tears away, dug in the equipment, and found the little pack of salts.

Everything was terrible, but Desiree understood terrible. She had lived through terrible her entire life, so she could handle this.

The only path was forward.

She climbed out of the ambulance past the dying man and rushed back over to Arthur. She waved the pack under his nose and he came back to reality with a gasp, eyes going wide. He grabbed her arm, steadying himself.

"What…what the hell…?"

"Relax," she said, making soothing noises. "Take a breath."

Arthur blinked and shook his head. "What the hell happened?"

"No clue," she said. "But I'm pretty sure this wasn't the plan."

He sat up. "Where's Niccolo? Jeremy?"

"I think Niccolo went inside the hospital. No clue where Jeremy is."

"Who started the fire?"

"The car?" she asked, smoke pouring out the front doors. "Oh."

"Help me up," Arthur said, climbing to his feet. "Did you stop the broadcast?"

"It's taken care of. They are still recording, but nothing is going out from here."

"Good. We can handle the rest. I'll go find Niccolo. You help settle things out here if you can."

He winced as he stood up, clutching his side.

"Will you be alright?" she asked.

"No," he said. "But there's no other choice. Just do your best."

"OK."

Arthur picked up his tranquilizer gun, tucked it into his belt, and then headed into the hospital. Desiree watched him go and then turned back to the riot happening around her.

She had no idea where to even start trying to fix this mess.

***

Niccolo moved into the emergency department, following the blood droplets. They headed off to the left down a hallway.

"Jeremy!" Niccolo shouted, moving after the boy and the injured girl. It was almost like there was ... smoke? "Stop running! She needs help."

He could smell something burning from up ahead and there was a little bit of smoke in the air. He heard gunshots from up ahead, a scream, and then a door slammed shut around a corner. He hurried forward to the corner, afraid of what he would find.

When he rounded it he saw two swat members in the hallway, one clutching his stomach and the other his leg. Used shotguns lay on the ground around them and neither of them were paying attention to him.

Niccolo saw bloody handprints smeared around a nearby door. He rushed over to it and saw that the droplet trail led down toward the basement. Alarm lights were blinking in the stairwell, disorienting him further.

"Jeremy!" he shouted, heading down the cement stairs after the kids. His mind was still muddled and he had to cling on the railing to keep his balance.

He coughed. It was coming from down below, billowing up in little clouds.

He covered his face with his shirt and kept going down the stairs, following the trail of blood. He only had one shot in his tranquilizer gun.

He staggered to the doorway at the bottom. Smoke was pouring out around the cracks, and he saw more blood on the handle.

The metal was warm to the touch but the fire wasn't very strong yet. Niccolo pulled the door open using the sleeve of his coat. A huge cloud of smoke billowed out past him, and he ducked low to the ground.

Inside was a large room full of barrels and machinery.

That fuel, Niccolo saw, was stored in plastic barrels stacked through the room. One of those barrels had been knocked over and cut, and the fuel inside was on fire.

Off to the right he saw two forms moving through the smoke, staying low to the ground. One was leaning on the other and he knew it was Jeremy and the little girl. They were about fifteen feet in front of him.

"Jeremy," he shouted, coughing. "Stop this madness! There is nowhere to go!"

The two forms stopped moving and one turned

back.

"I didn't do this!" Jeremy shouted. "This wasn't me."

"She's hurt because of you!" Niccolo yelled back. He raised his tranquilizer gun to fire, but just at that moment the flames burned through another nearby plastic barrel. The fuel splashed out, igniting quickly as the fire spread.

Another barrel followed suit, and then another, and within seconds the flames had tripled in size and scale. Niccolo pulled the trigger, but he could barely see anything through the smoke and couldn't be sure if he hit Jeremy or not.

He could have sworn, for only a second, that he saw two other forms in the smoke near the children, but they were gone just as fast, hidden in the smoke. His eyes must have been playing tricks on him.

He crawled further into the room, moving forward. He stayed low, covering his mouth with the neckline of his shirt, and struggled just to stay conscious. He reached something through the smoke as his hand fell upon a leg. He felt around the area and found the little girl on the ground, unconscious but alive.

Jeremy, though, he didn't find. He circled the area, trying to peer through the smoke, but it was impossible to see anything.

He grabbed the unconscious girl and dragged her back through the smoke. His breathing was shallow and weak. He made it back to the stairs and started crawling his way up, coughing with every step.

His vision clouded, but he pushed on, struggling to stay awake. They were almost out, only a few stairs left to go. A little farther ... a little farther ...

Everything went black.

∗∗∗

Desiree ripped open another gauze pack and handed it to the paramedic. They were running out of supplies, but the injuries were endless. Everything was still chaotic, but something had changed. No one was fighting anymore, and the civilians had blank looks in their eyes as they tried to understand what was happening.

Doctors and nurses in scrubs and lab coats milled around in confusion, splattered in blood and practically delirious. Some of them jumped back into action the way they had trained, saving lives, but it was clear that there would be more dead people than living by the time all of this was sorted out.

She heard the sounds of a tire squealing off to the right and saw a vehicle tear out from the side of the hospital. It was a white paneled van, and it was in one hell of a hurry. She watched it go, frowning, and then turned her attention back to helping the paramedic.

Arthur was carrying Niccolo over his shoulder and the girl under his arm, grimacing in pain. He brought them both over to where Desiree and the paramedic were, and wordlessly the man started working on her.

"What happened to Niccolo?" Desiree asked.

"Smoke inhalation," Arthur explained. "He'll be fine."

"Jeremy?"

"No sign of him. What happened out here?"

"A lot, but it looks like the fighting is over. "Now it is just time to pick up the pieces."

Arthur sat down next to her, surveying the devastation. Fire trucks could be heard in the distance.

"I suppose, then, that it's time to get back to work. There's a lot to clean up."

Epilogue

Niccolo came back to reality gasping and sputtering. He coughed, and it felt like he was hacking up an entire lung. His entire body was riddled with pain and his mind was hazy. He sat up too quickly and that was followed by another long fit of coughing that lasted a full thirty seconds.

He felt a hand patting him on the back, helping to clear his airways. He glanced around, somewhat panicked, and saw that Arthur was standing next to him. They were outside of the hospital, no longer in the basement where he last remembered being.

"Breathe," Arthur said, speaking softly. "Just breathe."

The coughing fit finally subsided, and Niccolo fell back. He was laid out on a hospital gurney in the back of an ambulance, though he had no clue how he'd gotten there.

The smell of smoke and ash hung in the air and it looked like daylight outside. He wracked his memories, trying to piece it all together. The last thing he remembered was crawling up the staircase, carrying the unconscious girl. There were clouds of smoke and he was near the exit, but he was almost positive he hadn't made it.

"What happened?"

"I got the crap kicked out of me," Arthur said with a laugh. "Pretty sure I broke a rib. Maybe two."

"I mean to me. How did I get back up here?"

"When I woke up, I saw you running into the hospital like a bat out of hell so I went in after you. Found you on the stairs leading to the basement, passed out. I dragged you out."

"What about the girl? Is she alright?"

"The paramedic thinks so, but it's impossible to know just yet. She is en route to another hospital about an hour away for surgery. She lost a lot of blood and went into shock from the bullet, but they are trying to stabilize her. The firefighters are still clearing the building, but most of the fuel already burnt itself out."

"What about the demons? Jeremy's army?"

"They just stopped," Arthur said, speaking quietly now. He glanced around to make sure no one was eavesdropping on them. "When I got you back up here everyone was done attacking each other and just trying to fix things up. All of the civilians are in custody, and none of them seem to remember what they did. Seven dead in total and no one seems to know what actually happened here."

"Jeremy," Niccolo said, letting out a sigh. "Without Jeremy, the demons couldn't hold onto the vessels.

"I didn't find him. Was he down there with you?"

"He's dead. He was in the basement with the flames, and there's no way he made it out alive."

Arthur was silent for a moment. "Are you certain he's dead?"

"He was in the basement with us. There's no way he got out of those flames and smoke."

"That settles it, then."

"The Vatican isn't going to be happy."

"We saved one of the children, and if my guess is correct we saved the right one. I think she is redeemable. With Jeremy... I'm not so sure."

"What about the recording equipment? They were recording all of this, weren't they? The cars, the fight, everything?"

"They were live streaming things as they happened.

At least, they thought they were. Desiree broke their satellite uplink, so as far as anyone outside this parking lot knows the connection dropped with all of the major networks before anything went down. As for the recordings, government officials are going to seize the tapes and send them to the Vatican."

Niccolo nodded. "Good." He let out a groan and started coughing again. Arthur handed him a glass of water and he took a sip. His mouth tasted like ash and smoke.

He was thoroughly exhausted, barely able to keep his eyes open. He closed his eyes and let out a yawn. "I think I'm going to go back to sleep."

"Good plan. I'll be back to check on you," Arthur replied, patting him on the arm.

"Sure thing," Niccolo said.

It only took seconds for Niccolo to fall back into a quiet slumber.

✳✳✳

Arthur waited impatiently for the fire department to finally clear out the blaze. They radioed in trucks from every nearby precinct, and by the time it was over with it was well into the next morning.

The hospital was still smoldering but the flames were out. About half of the building was damaged by the fire, but the other half was mostly untouched except for some smoke damage.

As the sun came up Arthur combed through the wreckage. Niccolo was probably right and Jeremy was dead, but he needed to be sure. He couldn't afford to tell the church the wrong thing.

Niccolo's assessment was confirmed, however,

after only a while of combing through the rubble. They found the burnt remains of a child in the basement. They couldn't verify an exact age or identity so early into the investigation, but Arthur knew exactly who it was.

Frieda arrived with Abigail only a short while later. She looked wary and a little bit afraid, but he assumed she was just surprised at how things went down. She left Abigail in the car and came out to meet him.

"It wasn't me," he said, smiling at her as she approached.

She didn't smile back. "What happened?"

He explained what went down as best as he could recall. Frieda listened to him patiently. "Operatives will be arriving in a few hours to clean the story up and smooth everything over," she said. "But for all intents and purposes it is over with."

"We lost Jeremy."

"The church will understand."

"What about the other children?"

"Most of them are already rounded up. A few more on the loose but we haven't had any new reports in about a day."

Her tone surprised him. "What's wrong?"

Frieda hesitated. She glanced over her shoulder. "We need to talk."

Frieda explained what had happened to her back in Minnesota. Curtis was an empath, and whatever Abigail had done to him, she hadn't meant to do it.

"What are you thinking?" he asked once she was finished.

"If he tells the church —"

"There's nothing to tell," he interrupted, defensive. "You said so yourself."

"Arthur," Frieda said gently, reaching out and touching his arm. "I'm with you on this. All I'm saying is that if he tells the Church what happened, there will be questions. Right now, though, the Church has bigger fish to fry in cleaning up this mess. As long as Abigail isn't with me, I can honestly say I don't know anything."

"What are you saying?"

"I'm saying: you're her father, and her guardian. It's your job to answer questions...and, if you are busy and difficult to track down..."

"They approved the adoption?"

"Yes. I already ran the paperwork and put it in the system. You are her father now."

He nodded, a little awestruck. The words made him feel like he was in a daze. "Alright. Is she ready to go?"

"We abandoned most of our stuff, but you can take her on a shopping trip to get caught back up."

"Alright."

"Are you going to take her home?"

Arthur hesitated, and then shook his head. "No. When I went back, it wasn't as bad as I expected, but I still won't raise her there. That was another life."

"Your cabin, then?"

"Most likely. How is she handling things?"

"Well enough. Better than me. I'll finish cleaning up this mess and get Niccolo's story. I think its best that you get back on the road and lay low for a while. Take my car, and I'll call you when I have another job."

Arthur nodded. "Thank you, Frieda."

He knew she was going out on a limb to do this. She should be reporting this information to the Council and the Vatican, not to him. The fact that she was willing to risk her career and her life took him a little by surprise, but he definitely appreciated it.

She started to turn away, but stopped. She turned back and gave him a quick hug, squeezing him close.

"Take care of her," Frieda said. "She needs you."

Then she headed off. Arthur watched her go with mixed feelings. His entire body ached and his back was throbbing from being tossed into the car, but the biggest thing he felt right now was trepidation.

Arthur watched her go and then turned back to the car where Abigail was sitting. She was staring at him with her big eyes and a hesitant look on her face. He was going to be a father again.

The idea terrified him.

✱✱✱

"Will he be alright?"

George Castinella gave the man a sharp and disapproving look. The man was bald, dirty, and disgusting to look at. His smell was a lot worse. The entire salvage yard smelled terrible, in fact. Rancid and rotten.

"He will be fine," he said, if only to shut his underling up. The truth was that George wasn't sure if Jeremy would survive. The arrogant little boy had inhaled a lot of smoke in that basement before they were able to pull him out, and he had been unconscious for the last two days. George had started the fire as a distraction, but it all had taken longer than he would have liked.

Jeremy was young, though, and children were resilient. He would more than likely recover, and when that happened George would be ready. He had bound his wrists and blindfolded him. If he couldn't see anyone, he couldn't control anyone.

The boy was lying on a cot in the backroom of the office, and he had been unconscious for the last day. He was covered in soot and dirt, a modest amount of which had already been washed away. He was still breathing, though, which was the important thing.

George stared at him with a slight smile curling his lip. Jeremy had been allowed his fantasy of redemption: George had done his part even though he knew it was a foolish plan, and now he would finish what he had started so many months ago when he first began working with the Bishop.

George's plan, which he'd spent weeks convincing the Bishop to support, was much more targeted and would result in greater impact. None of the children, Jeremy in particular, would have been wasted on such a pointless endeavor.

Now, he would train Jeremy as a weapon, something he could use to serve the cult's purpose. Together, they would bring the world to its knees.

This time around, though, Jeremy wouldn't have a say in the matter.

"He'll wake up," George said. "And, with him, we will set the world on fire."

About the Author

Lincoln Cole is a Columbus-based author who enjoys traveling and has visited many different parts of the world, including Australia and Cambodia, but always returns home to his pugamonster, Luther, and wife. His love for writing was kindled at an early age through the works of Isaac Asimov and Stephen King, and he enjoys telling stories to anyone who will listen.

The World on Fire Series

Raven's Peak

"Reverend, you have a visitor."

He couldn't remember when he fell in love with the pain. When agony first turned to pleasure, and then to joy. Of course, it hadn't always been like this. He remembered screaming all those years ago when first they put him in this cell; those memories were vague, though, like reflections in a dusty mirror.

"Open D4."

A buzz as the door slid open, inconsequential. The aching *need* was what drove him in this moment, and nothing else mattered. It was a primal desire: a longing for the tingly rush of adrenaline each time the lash licked his flesh. The blood dripping down his parched skin fulfilled him like biting into a juicy strawberry on a warm summer's day.

"Some woman. Says she needs to speak with you immediately. She says her name is Frieda."

A pause, the lash hovering in the air like a poised snake. The Reverend remembered that name, found it dancing in the recesses of his mind. He tried to pull himself back from the ritual, back to reality, but it was an uphill slog through knee-deep mud to reclaim those memories.

It was always difficult to focus when he was in the midst of his cleansing. All he managed to cling to was the name. *Frieda.* It was the name of an angel, he knew. . . or perhaps a devil.

One and the same when all was said and done.

She belonged to a past life, only the whispers of which he could recall. The ritual reclaimed him, embraced him with its fiery need. His memories were nothing compared to the whip in his hand, its nine tails gracing his flesh.

The lash struck down on his left shoulder blade, scattering droplets of blood against the wall behind him. Those droplets would stain the granite for months, he knew, before finally fading away. He clenched his teeth in a feral grin as the whip landed with a sickening, wet slapping sound.

"Jesus," a new voice whispered from the doorway. "Does he always do that?"

"Every morning."

"You'll cuff him?"

"Why? Are you scared?"

The Reverend raised the lash into the air, poised for another strike.

"Just...man, you said he was crazy...but this..."

The lash came down, lapping at his back and the tender muscles hidden there. He let out a groan of mixed agony and pleasure.

These men were meaningless, their voices only echoes amid the rest, an endless drone. He wanted them to leave him alone with his ritual. They weren't worth his time.

"I think we can spare the handcuffs this time; the last guy who tried spent a month in the hospital."

"Regulation says we have to."

"Then you do it."

The guards fell silent. The cat-o'-nine-tails, his friend, his love, became the only sound in the roughhewn cell, echoing off the granite walls. He took

a rasping breath, blew it out, and cracked the lash
again. More blood. More agony. More pleasure.

"I don't think we need to cuff him," the second
guard decided.

"Good idea. Besides, the Reverend isn't going to
cause us any trouble. He only hurts himself. Right,
Reverend?"

The air tasted of copper, sickly sweet. He wished he
could see his back and the scars, but there were no
mirrors in his cell. They removed the only one he had
when he broke shards off to slice into his arms and legs.
They were afraid he would kill himself.

How ironic was that?

"Right, Reverend?"

Mirrors were dangerous things, he remembered
from that past life. They called the other side, the
darker side. An imperfect reflection stared back,
threatening to steal pieces of the soul away forever.

"Reverend? Can you hear me?"

The guard reached out to tap the Reverend on the
shoulder. Just a tap, no danger at all, but his hand
never even came close. Honed reflexes reacted before
anyone could possibly understand what was
happening.

Suddenly the Reverend was standing. He hovered
above the guard who was down on his knees. The man
let out a sharp cry, his left shoulder twisted up at an
uncomfortable angle by the Reverend's iron grip.

The lash hung in the air, ready to strike at its new
prey.

The Reverend looked curiously at the man, seeing
him for the first time. He recognized him as one of the
first guardsmen he'd ever spoken with when placed in
this cell. A nice European chap with a wife and two

young children. A little overweight and balding, but well-intentioned.

Most of him didn't want to hurt this man, but there was a part—a hungry, needful part—that did. That part wanted to hurt this man in ways neither of them could even imagine. One twist would snap his arm. Two would shatter the bone; the sound as it snapped would be . . .

A symphony rivaling Tchaikovsky.

The second guard—the younger one that smelled of fear—stumbled back, struggling to draw his gun.

"No! No, don't!"

That from the first, on his knees as if praying. The Reverend wondered if he prayed at night with his family before heading to bed. Doubtless, he prayed that he would make it home safely from work and that one of the inmates wouldn't rip his throat out or gouge out his eyes. Right now, he was waving his free hand at his partner to get his attention, to stop him.

The younger guard finally worked the gun free and pointed it at the Reverend. His hands were shaking as he said, "Let him go!"

"Don't shoot, Ed!"

"Let him *go*!"

The older guard, pleading this time: "Don't piss him off!"

The look that crossed his young partner's face in that moment was precious: primal fear. It was an expression the Reverend had seen many times in his life, and he understood the thoughts going through the man's mind: he couldn't imagine *how* he might die in this cell, but he *believed* he could. That belief stemmed from something deeper than what his eyes could see. A terror so profound it beggared reality.

An immutable silence hung in the air. Both guards twitched and shifted, one in pain and the other in terror. The Reverend was immovable, a statue in his sanctuary, eyes boring into the man's soul.

"Don't shoot," the guard on his knees murmured. "You'll miss, and we'll be dead."

"I have a clear shot. I *can't* miss."

This time, the response was weaker. "We'll still be dead."

A hesitation. The guard lowered his gun in confused fear, pointing it at the floor. The Reverend curled his lips and released, freeing the kneeling guard.

The man rubbed his shoulder and climbed shakily to his feet. He backed away from the Reverend and stood beside the other, red-faced and panting.

"I heard you," the Reverend said. The words were hard to come by; he'd rarely spoken these last five years.

"I'm sorry, Reverend," the guard replied meekly. "My mistake."

"Bring me to Frieda," he whispered.

"You don't—" the younger guard began. A sharp look from his companion silenced him.

"Right away, sir."

"Steve, we should cuff..."

Steve ignored him, turning and stepping outside the cell. The Reverend looked longingly at the lash in his hand before dropping it onto his hard bed. His cultivated pain had faded to a dull ache. He would need to begin anew when he returned, restart the cleansing.

There was always more to cleanse.

They traveled through the black-site prison deep below the earth's surface, past neglected cells and through rough cut stone. A few of the rusty cages held prisoners, but most stood empty and silent. These prisoners were relics of a forgotten time, most of whom couldn't even remember the misdeed that had brought them here.

The Reverend remembered his misdeeds. Every day he thought of the pain and terror he had inflicted, and every day he prayed it would wash away.

They were deep within the earth, but not enough to benefit from the world's core heat. It was kept unnaturally cold as well to keep the prisoners docile. That meant there were only a few lights and frigid temperatures. Last winter he thought he might lose a finger to frostbite. He'd cherished the idea, but it wasn't to be. He had looked forward to cutting it off.

There were only a handful of guards in this section of the prison, maybe one every twenty meters. The actual security system relied on a single exit shaft as the only means of escape. Sure, he could fight his way free, but locking the elevator meant he would never reach the surface.

And pumping out the oxygen meant the situation would be contained.

The Council didn't want to bring civilians in on the secretive depths of their hellhole prison. The fewer guards they needed to hire, the fewer people knew of their existence, and any guards who were brought in were fed half-truths and lies about their true purpose. How many such men and women, he'd always wondered, knew who he was or why he was here?

Probably none. That was for the best. If they knew, they never would have been able to do their jobs.

As they walked, the Reverend felt the ritual wash away and he became himself once more. Just a man getting on in years: broken, pathetic, and alone as he paid for his mistakes.

Finally, they arrived at the entrance of the prison: an enclosed set of rooms cut into the stone walls backing up to a shaft. A solitary elevator bridged the prison to the world above, guarded by six men, but that wasn't where they took him.

They guided him to one of the side rooms, opening the door but waiting outside. Inside were a plain brown table and one-way mirror, similar to a police station, but nothing else.

A woman sat at the table facing away from the door. She had brown hair and a white business suit with matching heels. Very pristine; Frieda was always so well-dressed.

"Here we are," the guard said. The Reverend didn't acknowledge the man, but he did walk into the chamber. He strode past the table and sat in the chair facing Frieda.

He studied her: she had deep blue eyes and a mole on her left cheek. She looked older, and he couldn't remember the last time she'd come to visit him.

Probably not since the day she helped lock him in that cell.

"Close the door," Frieda said to the guards while still facing the Reverend.

"But ma'am, we are supposed to—"

"Close the door," she reiterated. Her tone was exactly the same, but an undercurrent was there. Hers was a powerful presence, the type normal people obeyed instinctually. She was always in charge, no matter the situation.

"We will be right out here," Steve replied finally, pulling the heavy metal door closed.

Silence enveloped the room, a humming

emptiness.

He stared at her, and she stared at him. Seconds slipped past.

He wondered how she saw him. What must he look like today? His hair and beard must be shaggy and unkempt with strands of gray mixed into the black. He imagined his face, but with eyes that were sunken, skin that was pale and leathery. Doubtless, he looked thinner, almost emaciated.

He was also covered in blood, the smell of which would be overpowering. It disgusted him; he hated how his daily ritual left him, battering his body to maintain control, yet he answered its call without question.

"Do you remember what you told me the first time we met?" the Reverend asked finally, facing Frieda again.

"We need your help," Frieda said, ignoring his question. "You've been here for a long time, and things have been getting worse."

"You quoted Nietzsche, that first meeting. I thought it was pessimistic and rhetorical," he continued.

"Crime is getting worse. The world is getting darker and..."

"I thought you were talking about something that might happen to someone else but never to me. I had no idea just how spot on you were: that you were prophesizing my future," he spoke. "Do you remember your exact words?"

"We need your help," Frieda finished. Then she added softer: "*I* need your help."

He didn't respond. Instead, he said: "Do you remember?"

She sighed. "I do."

"Repeat it for me."

She frowned. "When we first met, I said to you: 'Whoever fights monsters should see to it that in the process he does not become a monster.'"

He nodded. "You were right. Now I am a monster."

"You *aren't* a monster," she whispered.

"No," he said. "I am *your* monster."

"Reverend..."

Rage exploded through his body, and he felt every muscle tense. "That is *not* my name!" he roared, slamming his fist on the table. It made a loud crashing sound, shredding the silence, and the wood nearly folded beneath the impact.

Frieda slid her chair back in an instant, falling into a fighting stance. One hand gripped the cross hanging around her neck, and the other slid into her vest pocket. She wore an expression he could barely recognize, something he'd never seen on her face before.

Fear.

She was afraid of him. The realization stung, and more than a little bit.

The Reverend didn't move from his seat, but he could still feel heat coursing through his veins. He forced his pulse to slow, his emotions to subside. He loved the feeling of rage but was terrified of what would happen if he gave into it; if he embraced it.

He glanced at the hand in her pocket and realized what weapon she had chosen to defend herself. A pang shot through his chest.

"Would it work?" he asked.

She didn't answer, but a minute trace of shame crossed her face. He stood slowly and walked around the table, reaching a hand toward her. To her credit, she barely flinched as he touched her. He gently pulled her fist out of the pocket and opened it. In her grip was a small vial filled with water.

"*Will* it work?" he asked.

"Arthur..." she breathed.

The name brought a flood of memories, furrowing his brow. A little girl playing in a field, picking blueberries and laughing. A wife with auburn hair who watched him with love and longing as he played with their daughter. He quashed them; he feared the pain the memories would bring.

That was a pain he did not cherish.

"I need to know," he whispered.

He slid the vial from her hand and popped the top off. She watched in resignation as he held up his right arm and poured a few droplets onto his exposed skin. It tingled where it touched, little more than a tickle, and he felt his skin turn hot.

But it didn't burn.

He let out the shuddering breath he hadn't realized he was holding.

"Thank God," Frieda whispered.

"I'm not sure She deserves it," Arthur replied.

"We need your help," Frieda said again. When he looked at her face once more, he saw moisture in her eyes. He couldn't tell if it was from relief that the blessed water didn't work, or sadness that it almost had.

"How can I possibly help?" he asked, gesturing at his body helplessly with his arms. "You see what I am. What I've become."

"I know what you were."

"What I am no longer," he corrected. "I was ignorant and foolish. I can never be that man again."

"Three girls are missing," she said.

"Three girls are always missing," he said, "and countless more."

"But not like these," she said. "These are ours."

He was quiet for a moment. "Rescues?"

She nodded. "Two showed potential. All three were being fostered by the Greathouse family."

He remembered Charles Greathouse, an old and idealistic man who just wanted to help. "Of course, you went to Charles," Arthur said. "He took care of your little witches until they were ready to become soldiers."

"He volunteered."

"And now he's dead," Arthur said. Frieda didn't correct him. "Who took the girls?"

"We don't know. But there's more. It killed three of ours."

"Hunters?"

"Yes."

"Who?"

"Michael and Rachael Felton."

"And the third?"

"Abigail."

He cursed. "You know she wasn't ready. Not for this."

"You've been here for five years," Frieda said. "She grew up."

"She's still a child."

"She wasn't anymore."

"She's my child."

Frieda hesitated, frowning. He knew as well as she did what had happened to put him in this prison and what part Abigail had played in it. If Abigail hadn't stopped him...

"We didn't expect . . ." Frieda said finally, sliding

away from the minefield in the conversation.

"You never do."

"I'm sorry," Frieda said. "I know you were close."

The Reverend—Arthur—had trained Abigail. Raised her from a child after rescuing her from a cult many years earlier. It was after his own child had been murdered, and he had needed a reason to go on with his life. His faith was wavering, and she had become his salvation. They were more than close. They were family.

And now she was dead.

"What took them? Was it the Ninth Circle?"

"I don't think so," she said. "Our informants haven't heard anything."

"A demon?"

"Probably several."

"Where did it take them?" he asked.

"We don't know."

"What is it going to do with them?"

This time, she didn't answer. She didn't need to.

"So you want me to clean up your mess?"

"It killed three of our best," Frieda said. "I don't...I don't know what else to do."

"What does the Council want you to do?"

"Wait and see."

"And you disagree?"

"I'm afraid that it'll be too late by the time the Council decides to act."

"You have others you could send."

"Not that can handle something like this," she said.

"You mean none that you could send without the Council finding out and reprimanding you?"

"You were always the best, Arthur."

"Now I am in prison."

"You are here voluntarily," she said. "I've taken care of everything. There is a car waiting topside and a jet idling. So, will you help?"

He was silent for a moment, thinking. "I'm not that man anymore."

"I trust you."

"You shouldn't."

"I do."

"What happens if I say 'no'?"

"I don't know," Frieda said, shaking her head. "You are my last hope."

"What happens," he began, a lump in his throat, "when I don't come back? What happens when I become the new threat and you have no one else to send?"

Frieda wouldn't even look him in the eyes.

"When that day comes," she said softly, staring at the table, "I'll have an answer to a question I've wondered about for a long time."

"What question is that?"

She looked up at him. "What is my faith worth?"

***

The Reverend—Arthur, he reminded himself; his name was Arthur—sat on the red-velvet chair inside the private jet, high in the clouds and traveling at several hundred kilometers per hour. He felt out of place, sickened by the luxury and ostentation of this trip. He'd spent the last five years living in his roughhewn cell, and it had become his home.

He missed it, the cell with its lumpy mattress and low ceiling. It had become his sanctuary, a place to hide away from the world. Things had gotten to be too much for him to handle, and the utter simplicity of the cage took away his choices. It took away his free will and his ability to make mistakes.

Out here in the real world, mistakes were all he had left.

He looked out the window at the clouds and saw his face reflected there, but this time, it was more like the face he remembered. He'd shaved off the beard and cut his hair, and now he was wearing comfortable and light clothing. It would be cold in the mountains where he was heading, but he didn't fear the cold.

The onboard phone started to ring through a little speaker built into his chair. He stared at it curiously for a second and then pressed the green button to accept the call.

"Arthur?" Frieda asked as she was connected.

Her voice boomed through the jet's speakers, causing him to wince. He found the volume controls and turned it down to a more acceptable level. He hadn't realized just how peaceful his cell had been without loud noises.

"I'm here," he replied.

"You should be landing in just under an hour. We will have an escort ready to—"

"No escort," he said. "Just a car. I will travel alone."

"You should have someone with you in case—"

"No escort," he reiterated, cutting her off once more.

She was silent for a moment. "Very well," she agreed finally. "Did you find the supplies I left for you?"

He glanced at a cardboard box on the chair beside him with a frown on his face. "I did."

"I know it isn't much," she said, "but I can't make this trip common knowledge. I'm already pushing my luck with the jet."

It was definitely not much: a small caliber revolver, a few vials of holy water, a satellite phone, and a pair of short knives...none of the more powerful implements he'd used while he'd still been a Hunter serving the Council.

Then again, the one absolute thing he'd learned over the years was that those items had been a crutch. The only true weapon he'd had in his battles against evil had been his faith.

Something he'd lost long ago.

"You won't tell the Council?" he asked.

"No," Frieda replied. "They would never approve."

"How many of them wanted me dead when I went into the cell?"

"Arthur..."

"How many still do?" he asked.

She sighed. "They are fools for not trusting you."

"Maybe," he said. "Or maybe you're the fool."

She was silent for a long moment. "When you arrive at the airport we'll have a car waiting. The GPS is already set, and it's the last known coordinates of Rachael Felton's phone. It's up in the mountains out in the middle of nowhere."

"What were they doing there?"

"It isn't clear," Frieda said. "Rachael called us the day before she died and said she and her husband were chasing something powerful, and they said it was time sensitive as though it had an agenda. They picked up Abigail for backup and said they would report back to the Council once everything was taken care of. But they never did."

"So you sent a team?"

"The Council sent a team to check on them," Frieda

corrected. "And when they found the bodies…"

"You came to me," he finished.

"The Council is still debating its next steps. They think Rachael acted rashly by not calling for more backup, and they're trying to blame this on her. By the time they make a decision it will be too late."

"All right, Frieda," Arthur said. "I'm doing this for Abi. But you need to make sure my cell is ready for me when I get home."

***

As soon as the jet landed, Arthur stretched out his body and breathed in the cool mountain air. He allowed himself a few seconds to savor it before walking toward the waiting car. The airfield was empty except for his jet.

There were a few people watching him in suits, but they said nothing as he approached. He ignored their mixed expressions of awe and hatred and climbed into the waiting car

He had spent seven hours trapped on that jet being flown halfway across the world to the Rocky Mountains. The sun hadn't yet risen in the sky by the time he landed. The red, ominous glow in the clouds warned him that a storm was approaching, but he didn't have time to wait around.

He headed off into the mountains, following the GPS, and for the next several hours lost himself in the simple act of driving. It had been so long since he'd sat behind a steering wheel that it was almost cathartic.

He was forced to park alongside the road in a ditch and make the last leg of his journey on foot. It was a five mile hike into a cold and dark forest. His body burned from the exertion, and he loved the sensation. The walk gave him time to clear his mind and prepare himself for what he might find.

He didn't need the GPS to tell him that he'd arrived at the right location.

The bodies were torn to shreds, dried blood everywhere. Arthur could tell immediately, however, that the Council's foot soldiers had been mistaken about how many people were killed here in this clearing.

There were only two bodies.

It was a forgivable error with how mangled and disfigured those two were. He stood in a clearing, miles from civilization in any direction. Organs hung from tree limbs, entrails were ripped apart and scattered across the ground, and both heads were missing.

More than that, neither of the two heads were Abigail's, nor any dismembered body parts her shade of skin. She wasn't lying here mixed in with the dead, which meant she might still be alive.

She might be alive...

He had come here full of hatred, wanting nothing more than to avenge his adopted daughter and destroy whatever had taken her life. Frieda had manipulated him, knowing he would agree to this mission because of his love for Abigail. They both knew he relished the opportunity to punish whatever creature had harmed her.

But, if Abigail was alive and there was even the *slightest* chance of saving her...

The realization gave Arthur pause, and he felt a stirring of something he hadn't experienced in a long time: hope.

The Reverend patted the loaner pistol at his side—

a snub nose revolver that looked like a peashooter—
and headed through the trees. He had a few other
implements with him, including the knife and a vial of
holy water, as well as the satellite phone, but he didn't
bring much else.

The phone was off for now: anything technological
had a tendency to fail around the supernatural and was
more of a burden than anything else. He'd considered
leaving it behind as well but decided to hang onto it. He
was supposed to report in every hour and give Frieda a
status update, but that definitely wasn't going to
happen. This wasn't about her, and it sure as hell
wasn't for her.

Instead, he followed the tracks.

Those tracks weren't even hidden: broken
branches, scraps of discarded clothing, and dried
blood. Arthur felt like he was being led somewhere
rather than chasing something. Never a good sign.
After killing two members of Arthur's order, this
demon had to know there would be retaliation.
Whatever Arthur was dealing with, it wasn't afraid of
him at all.

He walked for a few hours, stepping lightly and
feeling his body limber up as he went. The air tasted
perfect. He'd grown used to the stale oxygen from the
caves, piped in through the elevator shaft and having
an oily, metallic flavor. This air tasted of trees and
nature. He hadn't even known how much he missed
clean air, and he could feel it rejuvenating his soul.

He paused at a tree line looking over an empty
mining town. It was built into the side of a hill and
consisted of around twenty dilapidated buildings. The
tracks led him here, and he knew the demon was
somewhere in the town, waiting for him.

Squat houses that were rundown, decrepit, and overgrown with vines surrounded a broken down church. This was an old country-store town, abandoned in the woods and falling apart in the preceding years.

Four spikes adorned with heads were standing in front of the church. Each had an expression of horror and served as a deterrent: a warning.

He remembered how a sight like this would have bothered him when he was a younger man. Two of the heads were the missing Hunters, and the other two he didn't recognize. When he was younger, knowing that this creature had killed his friends would have made him furious enough to charge headlong into the church and start blasting everything in sight. The depravity of it would have bothered him.

The only thing that bothered him now was how little he cared.

A mist hung in the air as the sun rose, dew clinging to his boots. He felt a breeze of wind and tasted moisture. It was quiet in the clearing, filled with foreboding.

He walked through the overgrown street toward the church. Broken shutters and roof tiles littered the dirt road as he went. It felt like a ghost town: empty, uninviting, and threatening.

The sun flitted through the trees overhead. It was eerily quiet, not even birds or insects chirping. They could feel the supernatural presence, the sheer *wrongness* of it, as easily as he could. Even the forest could sense something was amiss.

The church was bigger up close, built on a hill and dwarfing the buildings around it. Part of the ceiling was caved in and it was covered in mold and vines. He guessed it to have been built in the middle of the nineteenth century. It must have been abandoned not long after.

He stepped past the spikes, barely noticing the grotesque expressions of pain and terror on the faces of his friends. He'd seen worse in his time.

He'd done worse in his time.

He moved to the door and slipped the snub nose revolver from his belt. It felt comfortable in his hand, ready and waiting to deal death.

The door was cracked. Inside, he heard the creaking of a board as someone strode across the floor.

"Whoever I find inside," he said, "I will kill."

A moment passed in silence, and then a silky, smooth voice came back to him. It was a voice he recognized instantly:

"That..."

The Reverend felt a shiver run down his spine and his heart skipped a beat. "No, no, no," he muttered.

The door opened smoothly in front of him and he saw Abigail standing there, a lascivious smile on her face.

"...would be a shame," she finished.

www.ingramcontent.com/pod-product-compliance
Lightning Source LLC
Chambersburg PA
CBHW060547190726
48283CB00003B/898